SEX AND SKATEBOARDS

Visit us at www.boldstrokesbooks.com

Sex and Skateboards

by
Ashley Bartlett

2011

SEX AND SKATEBOARDS

ISBN 10: 1-60282-562-9
ISBN 13: 978-1-60282-562-8

THIS TRADE PAPERBACK ORIGINAL IS PUBLISHED BY
BOLD STROKES BOOKS, INC.
P.O. BOX 249
VALLEY FALLS, NY 12185

FIRST EDITION: SEPTEMBER 2011

CREDITS
EDITOR: CINDY CRESAP
PRODUCTION DESIGN: SUSAN RAMUNDO
COVER PHOTO BY MEGAN TILLMAN
COVER DESIGN BY SHERI (GRAPHICARTIST2020@HOTMAIL.COM)

Acknowledgments

I can't skateboard. There, I said it. I can't surf either. But I've always been impressed by those who can. This is my nod to them.

Mom, Pam, Dad, thanks for keeping my bookshelves stocked with Nancy Drew when I was seven and Radclyffe when I was seventeen. I know I made raising me hard, but you guys always made growing up easy.

Mare, Jessica, Megan, thanks for reading all five hundred versions of this book. And, Mare, I'm sorry I told you all those commas were unnecessary. My bad.

Jack, thanks for always cooking dinner for me at midnight. Oh, and for that roof you put over my head. Maybe I'll let you read this book past the acknowledgements page now. Maybe not.

I also want to thank everyone at Bold Strokes. Thanks for taking a chance on me. And thanks for making this book so much better than it was. And, seriously, Cindy, I swear I'll learn proper grammar someday.

Dedication

For Meg

CHAPTER ONE

W hy was the sun so damn bright? I barely had sheets on my bed, let alone curtains. When pulling a pillow over my head failed to block the light, I decided to get up. My bed was in my living room, and it wasn't so much of a bed as a futon. Whatever. I was lucky I had gotten a place at all. Boxes littered the front room of the small house and I stumbled around them. Even though I was physically out of bed, I wouldn't be awake for hours. I still couldn't figure out why people got up early on purpose.

The only thing in the refrigerator was a container of orange juice. I took a healthy gulp straight from the carton. A week before, I'd found my French press broken in its box from the move. A complicated coffee machine was buried in one of the open boxes, but I didn't feel the need to look for it. I had yet to successfully operate the damn thing and was not up for trying, even today, when I was in such dire need for some Sumatran.

The sun pouring in my kitchen window was starting to look more appealing so I slid the glass door open and tentatively stepped onto the cold patio. My nipples instantly hardened. As an afterthought, I slipped on my Vans. If I climbed onto the pile of firewood stacked against the house, I could get on the roof. The house across the street was one of the few one-story places on the block, and it was the only thing between the water and me. The view was fucking awesome. The morning air smelled like the ocean, but it felt different here than what I was used to. San Francisco had the damp feel of the sea, but you practically had to be standing in the surf on Baker's Beach just to smell the salt. This place was like a real ocean.

The theme song from *Three's Company* went off in my pocket, abruptly bringing me back from my daydream.

"Hey, Ollie," I answered the phone.

"Wow, Alden, I didn't expect you to be awake," her exuberant voice greeted me.

"Just got up." I yawned and rubbed my eyes.

"I was just going to leave a message. Why aren't you sleeping?"

"I don't know. I'm not sure what the hell is wrong with me."

"I'm about to head down to the restaurant. The contractor said we could work in there now. Want to meet me?"

"Whatever you say, boss," I responded.

"Don't call me that. It's creepy." A playful note crept into her voice. "Besides, if you're annoying I'll just fire you."

"That'll happen. Listen I need a shower. Give me thirty minutes."

"Sounds good. See you then."

"Later." I hung up and slipped the phone back into my pocket.

Twenty minutes later, I slung my backpack over my shoulder and locked the front door of my house. It was just a guesthouse, but the owner rented both places out during the summer, and my place was far enough away to separate it from the main house. It was already an awesome day so I rode my skateboard down Pacific Ave into the center of town. I turned onto Ocean Front and let myself in the back door of the restaurant. Ocean Front was just like it sounded, one side of the road was the ocean and the other was the back of all the shops and restaurants on South Ocean, really just a glorified parking lot. I found Ollie in the dining room with her laptop and a cup of tea.

"Dude."

She turned around. "Hey, how's it going?"

I sat across from her at the table. "All right," I said as I dropped my bag on the floor.

"Here's all the numbers that you'll need. Alarm, wireless password, and our phone number." She slid a piece of notebook paper across the table to me. "And, hey, the sound system is getting installed today."

I glanced over the list as she talked. She also handed me a thick purple file folder. Ollie was big on colorful shit like that.

"These are all the applications we've gotten. I tagged the ones I think are promising with little pink sticky notes." That's what I was talking about. She loved to color code things. "And I put blue sticky notes on the ones that I thought were hilarious." I raised an eyebrow at her. "I know it's idiotic, but one of them misspelled California Polytechnic. So if you have time you should look them over."

"Okay, but I'm looking at the pink ones first. Can I start interviewing soon?"

Her eyes traveled from my face to my nipple and stared pointedly. The outline of the ring was pretty obvious through the thin T-shirt I was wearing.

"Fine, I'll put on a real shirt so it won't show. Do you want me to wear a pink tongue stud too?"

"The restaurant is named after my grandmother. I think you can manage to keep it PG." She didn't care about the piercings and we both knew it, so I just rolled my eyes at her. "Does this mean you're going to start acting like a big kid?"

"You never said when you gave me the job that I would have to act like an adult."

"Alden, you are an adult. I'm just waiting for you to catch on."

I shrugged in response. Ollie thought that my behavior was an act. I didn't and it was too nice of a day to fight.

We turned to our respective tasks and worked quietly. The silence started getting to me so I started iTunes on Ollie's laptop.

"In a couple hours we'll be able to play that on our very own stereo." Ollie did a little dance in her seat.

"Thanks for reiterating everything you've told me, Ollie. You know how my memory is going," I said without looking up from the file in front of me.

"Bitch." She smiled.

By the time I worked through the pink, the normal, and finally, the blue stack, I'd been sitting and staring at paper for way too long. Why the fuck did I take this job?

"Dude, I need coffee." I stood and stretched. "I'll start calling around when I get back."

"You just want to check out the hot girl who hangs out at Lucy's."

"Ollie, I would never." I was the picture of indignation. She scoffed. "It's not my fault. She's really, really hot." Normally I didn't linger in coffee shops to gawk at unbelievably attractive women. I didn't need to try that hard, and I'm not trying to sound conceited. If a chick was into me, that was cool, if not, I'd get over it. But this chick was too cool. I'm supposed to be the one who's too cool, who's laid back, which is a nice way of saying I'm lazy. Whatever.

"Hey, McKenna." I hated when she called me that. It brought me right back to ninth grade gym. "Don't take too long. And bring me some tea. The black one with the oranges."

"Whatever you say, boss," I called as I headed out the door.

❖

I went outside to wait for my drinks after ordering. The four tables on the sidewalk were all occupied. The two to the left of the door were pushed together to accommodate a group of hella old people. Why did seventy-year-olds travel in packs? On the right, a couple of sullen teenagers sprawled smoking and drinking coffee. Beyond the teenagers was the chick Ollie had been teasing me about. She was plugging a camera into the Mac in front of her. Not a little camera either, like a half-the-size-of-my-head-camera. I couldn't tell where she was looking because she was wearing these big dark glasses. Her long hair was tucked up under a trucker hat. Cayucos Surf Co., one of the local surf shops, was tagged in loud colors across it. Curly, honey-colored tendrils were falling out the sides. She was at most twenty-five, probably not even that, so I had at least a year on her. Studiously pretending not to watch her, I turned toward the geriatrics.

"Hey, Seth," the hot chick called to the teenager facing her. "Bum me a smoke."

"Sorry, Wes. Got mine from Kayla." He pointed to the girl sitting next to him.

"Kayla. Hook me up."

"I'm out. He took my last one." The girl tossed a pack onto the next table.

With annoyance, the hot girl flipped open the pack, and finding it lacking, tossed it back on the table.

"I've got one," I said.

"That would be awesome." Then she smiled. It was all white teeth and curving pink lips. She had a dimple on one cheek but not the other. My stomach dropped and resided heavily about six inches lower than it should.

"Here." I opened the pack and thumbed one out so she could take it. She extracted it with two long fingers.

"Can I get a light too?" she said with another one of those smiles. I handed her my lighter. She looked around as she lit the cigarette and realized all the tables were taken. "Hey, you want to sit? I don't mind sharing." She twirled the lighter and handed it back.

"Sure, thanks." I pulled out the chair across from her and sat down. "I'm Alden, by the way."

She closed her laptop. "Weston. Wes, actually."

I just grinned.

Weston smiled again. "You're new around here. Summer vacation?"

"Nope. My friend is opening a restaurant a couple doors down." I pointed to where the new sign for Delma's hung.

She turned to look where I was pointing. "Oh, that's Olivia Crawford's place, right?"

"Uh-huh. You know her?" I asked, surprised.

"We were junior lifeguards together for three summers." She laughed.

"I guess you're a local then, huh?" I grinned back.

"I guess."

I heard my drinks called from inside. "That's me. Just a sec." I retrieved my drinks then went back outside and sat.

"So you're here to help Olivia set up?"

"Kind of. I'm the executive chef."

Her lips formed a perfect O. She recovered pretty quickly. "Don't take this the wrong way, but aren't you a little young?"

That made me laugh. "Yeah, but I promise I'm older than I look. But Ollie just hired me to be nice. It's total charity because I'm not the most professional and I look like I'm twelve."

"No, no. You look at least thirteen." She managed a serious face when she said it. Now that was something to value in a girl. Sarcasm.

"Great. Thank you."

My phone rang. That ringtone was seriously embarrassing. "Sorry. It's Ollie." I flipped the phone open. "'Lo."

"Dude, you get lost?"

"Ha ha. No. But I met a friend of yours."

"Serious? Who?"

"Weston." I looked at Weston and waited for a last name.

"Duvall."

"Duvall," I repeated.

"Oh my God. Is she the hot chick you were drooling over?" Ollie started dying of laughter.

"All right, I'll be right over." What an ass. What if Weston could hear?

"Wait, wait," Ollie said between gasps for air. "Tell her I said hey."

"Sure, whatever." I snapped the phone shut and turned back to Weston. "I should head back. Ollie says hey."

"Tell her the same."

"I will." I stood and picked up the two paper cups. "Maybe I'll see you here again?"

"Probably. I'm here every day." Score.

I needed activity. I'd been in Cayucos for about a week, so I booted up my laptop and searched for skate parks. Should have done it before I even left SF. My search turned up two in San Luis, so I wrote down the locations, grabbed my board and a Red Bull, and left.

The first looked shady. A big group of guys in their late teens lounged in front of the fence. Shiny sneakers, jeans that were way too baggy, and general looks of disgust for anything and everything moving. Not a single skateboard between them. That meant this was the park for the dealers, which also meant it was the park to get the shit kicked out of you. Fuck that. Next.

The next park on my list had me praying. If it sucked, I'd have to get a baggy sweatshirt and look tough, but not too tough, and go back to the dealer park. I'd rather not have my skateboard swung at my head, because I'd seen that happen and you lose teeth, but I had to skate. No choice.

It was up on a hill so I parked and grabbed my skateboard. I crested the hill and peered through the metal fence. That was a motherfuckin' skate park. It was huge, entirely cement, with two massive bowls. At ground level surrounding the bowls, quarter pipes edged the park interspersed with rails and ramps that either dropped off into nothing or curved back to the ground. Sunlight glinted off the smooth white cement contrasting sharply with corners and edges that were waxed and scarred black. Perfect.

My timing was good because it was still early so the park was nearly empty. I rode around the outside of the bigger bowl getting a feel for the terrain. After finding the best route for speed, I set up across from the deepest section of the bowl. From my kick off point, I pushed hard over a mound in the center, around a bowl so I was nearly parallel to the ground, picking up speed before I entered the bowl I wanted. I crouched as I came up the wall. At the last second I tapped the tail of the board, slid my foot to the nose, and became airborne in a perfect ollie. Instead of spinning like I wanted it to, the board fell away from my Vans. My feet slammed hard into the ground and I fell back on my ass. Skating hurts. If nothing else, skaters had persistence. I tried again. And again. The fifth time, I got it. The wheels smacked down and continued rolling, with me on it no less. I whipped my head around because I was riding goofy now, effectively going backward. With an abrupt swivel of my hips and the proper shifting of my feet, I was skating normal again.

Back at the starting point, I did it again with an extra kick for speed. This time I was going 360. Nope, this time I was falling on my ass again. I let it happen and ended up on my back staring at the sun. So I picked my sorry ass up and went back to the beginning. I totally almost had it. Except I didn't. When I landed, I really screwed up. Only one foot landed on the board, dead center. It was already getting flimsy and that was the last straw. I felt more than heard the sharp telltale crack as the board gave way under me. Damn. There went skating for the day.

I lit a cigarette and picked up the pieces of my board. There was a dilapidated picnic table on the far side of the park. I crossed over and sat on the table with my feet on the bench. In between drags of my cigarette, I examined the spent board. The trucks were in decent condition so I could probably salvage them. But I'd already used them on two boards so I wanted new ones. The wheels were shot. Hell, I was in a new town. It was time for an all new setup.

Chapter Two

San Luis Obispo had a decent amount of skate shops. Most catered to the surfers, but there were still some cool places for skateboarders. On Monterey, I found a place with broken graffitied TVs in lieu of a window display. I was hooked. Inside had high ceilings and concrete everything. It was real clean, a little industrial. On the far left wall, a glass counter had all manner of wheels, trucks, and other skateboard necessities. Behind the counter, the entire wall was covered in skate decks. I found one I liked with thick black and white stripes. The kid behind the counter had to show me about twenty of the trucks in the case before I found some I liked. They were basic matte black with matching hardware. All the kids were into bright colors and crazy graphics, which were totally cool, but it detracted from the board. When I flew off a ramp and became airborne, I wanted people looking at the cool shit I could do, not at my gear. Lime green wheels were my only indulgence, and once they were fitted with the best bearings the shop carried, the kid behind the counter assembled my board.

When it was done, I tossed it to the ground. The impact made a sharp crack like the splintering of wood. I love that sound, the sound of a board slapping concrete. I stepped on, leaning back and forth to test it out.

"How does it feel?" he asked like he knew what he was talking about.

"It's all right. A little tight." I popped the back and slid my foot up to the nose in a small controlled ollie. "Feels good."

"You want me to loosen it up a bit?"

"Naw. It's cool."

"Sick." It totally was. "I love that deck. Real simple, ya know?" Maybe he did know what he was talking about.

After paying for my newly assembled board, I started down Monterey, testing out my toy. I cut down a side street and back up Higuera. The sidewalk wasn't too crowded, which was good because I didn't want to ride in the street. That's just asking to get taken out by a car. In the large windows facing the street, I checked myself out. I looked good. Up ahead of me, a door opened into the street. I swerved enough to avoid hitting it, but the trucks were too tight to miss the person who backed out the door straight into me. Hello, cement.

"Oh my God. I'm so sorry." My assailant knelt next to me.

I looked up into a pair of dark shades and grinned.

"Alden?" She seemed concerned.

"Hey, Weston." If I'm going to get taken out by someone, it better be a hot girl.

"Are you all right?"

"Yeah. You know? I think that's why you're not supposed to skate on a sidewalk." My stomach twisted in the good way when she smiled in response.

"Probably." She stood and offered a hand. I let her pull me into a standing position, surprised at her strength. "So why are you? Skating on a sidewalk, I mean."

"New skateboard." We both looked down at the upside down board. The wheels were still spinning. Good bearings.

"Cool."

"Thanks." With a motion I didn't even think about, I tapped a wheel with my foot so it would flip over, then popped the board into my hand. Ouch. My palm rubbed against the grip tape, making me realize that my hand was torn and bloody. "Fuck."

"Damn. You're hurt." Weston lifted my wrist to look at the damage.

"It's not bad." A drop of blood hit the ground between us.

"You've got to be kidding."

"What?" I shook my hand, flinging off any excess blood. Most of it was cement rash anyway.

"Don't act all tough."

"I'm not." She so wasn't buying it. "I get cut up all the time when I'm skating."

"Come on." Her hand closed around my wrist and she started up the sidewalk.

"Where are we going?" I caught up so she wouldn't be dragging me.

"To clean up your hand." We turned up a side street, a small one I wouldn't have noticed. It didn't have the big flashy windows of the main roads. She stopped at a large wood door, opened it, and motioned me inside. For about a second I considered that I didn't know her and I had no idea where I was anymore, then I walked inside. It was a coffee shop. The kid behind the counter scowled at us. That's what I value in a barista: disdain. It's so much more honest.

"What is this place?" The interior was poorly illuminated, and the dark wood interior that matched the door didn't help lighten it up.

"This is where the hipsters go." Her tone implied that it was only half a joke. "Bathroom is this way." I followed her down a corridor along the far wall and through another door. The bathroom matched the rest of the building. A bulb above the sink was the only light. The walls were dark red and covered in graffiti that ranged from call whoever for a good time to intricate sharpie murals of dragons and fairies. It was also one of the smallest bathrooms I'd ever been in.

"Interesting." I pretended to look at the art surrounding me. Really, I was just checking her out.

"I guess." Old news apparently. "Here." She flipped on the water and placed my bloody hand under the stream. I made a half-assed attempt not to press against her, but gave up pretty quickly. The bathroom was small. Serious.

"I did a photo shoot in here once."

"Really?" I wondered how that was possible.

"Uh-huh. My model was this pale, clean-looking girl, and I wanted to put her somewhere dirty." While she spoke, her fingers rubbed over my palm. Transfixed, I just stared and let her.

"That sounds cool."

"It turned out okay." When all the blood was off, she held my palm closer to the light to inspect the scrape. "This doesn't look too bad."

"Told you."

Wes turned off the water then methodically dried my hand. "Here. Hold these. I can't see." She slid the sunglasses off her face and handed them to me. Her eyes were such a bright blue-green that I would have been able to see them from twenty feet away. Suddenly, I knew. That bathroom was a trap. That coffee shop was a trap. Because all the air was sucked out of the room, and my lungs cried out. Instead of oxygen, my chest filled with her. The tangy, fruity scent of her hair, I couldn't identify what exactly, probably because my brain wasn't firing right. Her eyes, overflowing with color, washed over and through me. Between us, the air was stifling.

"Do you want…" she stuttered. Maybe it was the look in my eyes. "We should…" I held on to every word. She licked her lips. "Coffee? Can I get you a coffee?"

"Sure."

Weston licked her lips again. It was more of a sexy dart of pink tongue between her lips and a slow drag of her bottom lip into her mouth.

"You're, umm…the door."

"Right. Yeah." Careful not to touch her, I groped for the door handle behind me and tumbled out, spinning to face the room. She was still close behind me.

❖

Tuesday's interviews went decent. Wednesday was a nightmare. My first interview didn't know we were opening a restaurant. That was why I was supposed to do phone screens. My bad. The second flirted with me the entire time even though she was maybe fifteen. The third wasn't terrible. The fourth had a tattoo on his neck. I'm not judging, but I'm pretty sure it was a very anatomically correct woman. I tried not to stare. By twelve thirty, I was ready to kill myself. I had half an hour before the torture started again, so I went to Lucy's for more coffee.

Sitting on a bench halfway between Delma's and Lucy's, a familiar figure was working on a laptop. Today, Weston left the hat at home and tons of slightly curling warm blond hair cascaded over her shoulders and down her back.

"Hey." I came to a stop in front of her.

Weston looked up from her laptop. "Hey." She smiled. The moment passed for her to look away, and instead, her eyes dropped to my Vans and slowly climbed up my body. She was definitely cruising me. There was something else, though, like she was shaping me. Under her scrutiny I became what she wanted, what she saw.

I slid the cigarette from behind my ear and set it between my lips.

"What?" The unlit cigarette bobbed.

"Just stay there." Without looking away, she picked up a black box sitting next to her, just slightly too big for her hand, and cradled it facing me. Immediately, the device became a part of her. There was no moment of transition. It was as if she'd picked up a part of her, like her hand, or maybe her soul, and the two fused. It took a second for me to recognize that it was a camera, the thing had to be eighty years old. Deft fingers flipped up the top then slid to the side where I heard a click. She twisted a knob and stood dropping her sunglasses onto the bench.

"What are you doing?"

"What does it look like?" She moved around my side and I heard the click again. "Pretend I'm not here."

"That's difficult. We're standing in the middle of a sidewalk and you're taking pictures of me."

"Ignore it." The camera clicked twice more. Her face was a study in concentration. I felt a part of her, connected by the apparatus in her palm, and I wasn't sure why.

In an effort to ignore her as instructed, I shrugged and dug in my pocket for a lighter. Weston stepped up onto the bench so the camera was at the level of my shoulders. As I curled around my lighter and dipped my head to catch the flame, she clicked and twisted three more times in rapid succession. As suddenly as she'd started, she was done. The camera was placed on the worn wood that she now reclined against and she stretched her feet out across the sidewalk.

"So you're a photographer?" I pointed at the camera ingeniously.

"Yep." Her big sunglasses back in place, she crossed her arms over a Cayucos Surf Co. tank top. She was fuckin' built. She wasn't that tall and she was thin, but those arms. Damn. I was turned on and jealous all at the same time. No matter what I did, I was always scrawny. A lot of people thought I looked anorexic. Not this girl. She probably worked out or something, probably a health nut. "Can I have a cigarette?" Maybe not.

"Sure." I held the pack out to her and sat on the far side of the bench, her camera between us. "So what type of photography?"

"Thanks." She lit the cigarette. "I'm the artistic type." That was ambiguous. The end of her cigarette flared as she took a drag.

"Right."

"Oh, hey, is your hand okay?" She uncrossed her arms and leaned toward me.

"It's fine." I lifted the offending extremity. Scrapes covered the surface ranging from dark red to pink. "It just looks gross."

"I can't believe I did that." Somewhere between disgusted and impressed, she found her smile.

"Technically, it's my fault. I was the idiot riding a skateboard on the sidewalk."

"I still knocked you on your ass."

"Could you say it a bit louder please? I still have some of that pesky dignity left." I grinned at her.

"Don't be such a girl about it or I'll have to knock you on your ass again."

"Anytime you like." Seriously.

"So when is the restaurant going to open?"

"July, hopefully. Ollie has most of her renovations finished so they're actually letting us in the building. At this point, we just need staff. I'm doing interviews most of today."

"Fun."

"Oh, it's a blast," I replied sarcastically. "One guy I interviewed had tits tattooed on his neck."

"Was it a guy named Georgie?"

"Dude, you know him?" Did everyone know each other here?

"Yeah, nice guy. Dumb as hell, but nice. You know Jamie that works at Lucy's?" She pointed down the street. "He's her brother."

"No way. I guess she got the good side of the uterus."

"Pretty much." When she laughed, smoke poured from her mouth.

"Is he any good?"

She shrugged. "He's a good cook." He was hired. I'd do anything she said. I had a hopeless crush and we'd only talked three times. "So any other interesting interviews?"

"They're all interesting. Idiots, but they're interesting." I shrugged. "Maybe my one o'clock will go better."

"One o'clock?" She looked at her watch.

"What time is it?" Damn. I didn't even get coffee yet.

"Four 'til." She was trying not to smile.

"Fuck." I stood. "See you later." I took off down the street sketching a wave in the air behind me.

"Later," she called.

Chapter Three

My new sous-chef was hella cool. Ollie was pissed I'd ditched out on picking up her cousin with her at the train station, but I had to show Cliff around like right then. I spent almost two hours giving him the tour and finishing his paperwork. It should have only taken an hour or so, but we kept getting sidetracked. I liked the guy a lot. Ollie called somewhere around the hour and a half mark and said they were on their way. I was just showing Cliff out the back when she called again. They were waiting for me at Lucy's. I locked up and headed down the street.

"'Sup, bitch," Lauren yelled when I was within sight.

"Slut." Who didn't love being called inappropriate pet names? Especially at top volume.

"Where the hell have you been?"

"I'm working this shit job for your cousin and I had to pick up her slack." I sauntered closer.

Ollie was standing behind her. "Thanks for that, by the way." She gave me a head nod.

"Yeah, yeah." It was odd to see them standing there together. Sure, I saw them together all the time. They just happened to be dressed similarly, which made them look even more alike. Both had this pale skin that never tanned or burned, and long, dark hair that fell into their eyes when they concentrated or got mad. The only difference was that Lauren was shorter. Ollie and I each had a couple inches on her. Hey, at least if I lost one, I had a backup.

I got closer and Lauren threw herself onto me. She wrapped her arms around my neck and mine went around her waist. We turned in a half circle from her momentum.

"I missed you." She kissed my cheek.

"Whatever." Most people thought Lauren and I were together or something because we acted like that. We weren't. We just weren't into each other that way. She was hot in a Banana Republic kind of way. I was more into skate jeans and less into sweater vests, unless it was a cool sweater vest.

"So are we getting coffee?" It was the only thing to do in this town. I slung my arm around Lauren's shoulders and leaned against her.

"Yeah. I need some tea to settle my stomach after watching you and my baby cousin." Ollie glared at me in a very unconvincing way.

"Just because you're attracted to boys doesn't mean you need to look down on our love, Olivia Crawford." Lauren turned up her nose at her. "Come on, doll face." She grabbed my hand and pulled me inside Lucy's. I hated when she called me that.

I looked out the big window at Ollie who was pretending to retch on the sidewalk. Very mature. Just past her a black Volvo parked and Weston angled out of it. I tried to remove my arm from Lauren's neck. She still had a death grip on my arm though. The more I pulled away, the tighter her grip got. We started wrestling subtly. Ollie and Weston filed into the coffee shop.

"Hey, Weston." I grinned. My two best friends were in town, one of which nearly had me in a headlock, and I was looking at the hottest chick I had ever seen in real life. My day was definitely going well. Lauren and Weston started sizing each other up. Weird.

"Lauren, this is Weston. Weston, this is Lauren. She's Ollie's cousin." They said the appropriate things. Lauren gave me the approving eye. Weston was scowling at Lauren who finally released me so that she could order a drink. I tossed a twenty on the counter and asked the barista to throw Weston's drink on our tab.

"You want a cigarette?" I asked Weston. Ollie was still deciding what to get.

"Sure," Weston said as we walked outside. "You didn't have to do that, you know."

"I know." I held my cigarettes out to her.

"Thanks." She took the pack and my lighter. "So how long is your friend in town?" When she said friend it sounded decidedly unfriendly.

"I don't know. A couple days, maybe a week." We snagged the big table. She sat next to me.

"Oh." We smoked in silence for a while with our legs stretched out on the sidewalk. I studied my cigarette.

"So we're all going to San Luis tonight to hit up that, umm, market thing if you, umm, want to come." That was stupid. I barely knew her.

"Thanks, but I'm kind of busy." Yep, that was pretty clear.

"That's cool." I nodded and resumed my cigarette examination.

"Make sure you get some Cal Poly eggs."

"Huh? Like the school? Why does the school have eggs?"

"It's an ag school. The students sell eggs at Thursday Night Market. They're the best." Weston leaned forward. She was getting seriously excited about these eggs.

"Eggs?"

"You think I'm crazy." She put up her hands and reclined again.

"No, I'll check out the eggs." I don't think she was convinced. We fell into silence as Lauren and Ollie joined us.

"All right, what's the plan?" Lauren leaned over me and stole a cigarette. Ollie and I looked at each other. We didn't have a plan.

"It's your party." I handed Lauren my lighter.

"I'm hungry. Let's drop off my stuff and get some food."

"Works for me." I stood and shoved my cigarettes into my back pocket.

"Thanks for the coffee, Alden." Weston saluted me with her paper cup.

"Anytime."

"Come on, doll face," Lauren shouted as she and Ollie moved toward the car.

I braced one hand on the table and leaned closer to Weston. "Are you sure you don't want to come?"

"I can't, but thank you." She looked sincere so I nodded and followed my friends to the car.

❖

When we got back from San Luis, it felt like a John Waters kind of night so we did *Desperate Living* then *Serial Mom*. Around three, Ollie went upstairs to crash. Lauren and I talked for another couple hours, mostly debating whether Mole from *Desperate Living* was hot. Eventually, she crashed too. I waited another half hour to make sure she was out 'cause I didn't want to wake her. I made sure her feet were covered with the blanket and set her glasses on the coffee table. Then I went to steal some of her clothes. Walking on the beach in jeans sucks. I found some cutoff khakis and Lauren's favorite sweatshirt. Once I was on the porch, I put my shoes on and tugged the hood up in an attempt to keep the cold out.

The ride down North Ocean was mellow. The sun was barely starting to show on the ridge to my left. There were no indications of life other than the sounds of my skateboard wheels reverberating back to me. When I hit the empty parking lot in front of the water, I put my shoes in my backpack and buckled my skateboard onto it. With my first step on the beach, my feet sank in. The sand was ice. The cold traveled up until I could feel it in my fingertips. I hurried to the water's edge where the ground was at least solid.

What struck me was the smell, or lack thereof. It didn't have the overwhelming odor of the ocean anymore. Almost like I had lived there long enough for the scent to be lost on me. Instead, I could smell damp grass and the dull bitterness of anise and wild mustard. The air was light and cool. No harsh wind. Morro Rock was in the distance to my left, and the pier stretched out to my right. I turned toward Morro. My place was this direction, as were the majority of the houses in Cayucos. Most of the houses on the beachside of Pacific Ave had staircases that led to the sand. In between the staircases, miniature caves were carved into the rock, a result of the ocean beating on the cliff for centuries. That was where I found her.

Weston was sitting with her arms wrapped around her legs. Her back was against a cement staircase and she was staring into one of the crevices. She was wearing board shorts and a Cayucos Surf Co. sweatshirt. I was pretty sure they were paying her for advertising at this point.

"You know, traditionally, when people sit on the beach they look at the ocean," I called.

Weston looked at me and smiled. "I'm not a traditional sort of girl." Even in the early morning light, her eyes shone. I stopped and stared.

"Alden?" I realized she was saying something to me.

"Huh?"

"What are you doing out here?"

"I could ask the same of you." I sauntered closer.

She shrugged. "Couldn't sleep. Now you go."

"After we went to Thursday Night Market, we stayed up all night, but they fell asleep, so here I am."

"Weird. It must be a sleepover night." She motioned a thumb over her shoulder up the stairs. "One of my friends has taken over my guest room too."

"Wait, that's your house? Damn." I backed up to get a better look. It was a huge two-story house all dark wood and windows. "Who the hell do you take pictures for?"

Weston started laughing. "Oh, it's not mine. It's more of a family property."

"Gotcha. Sooo you want to walk with me?" I nodded up the beach in the direction I was going.

"Sure," she said with a quick glance back at the house before settling her gaze on me again. "I think Trevor can handle waking up without me."

"I'm sure he can. Come on." I grabbed her hand and pulled her along with me. Surprisingly, she didn't let go. "So why is he crashed in your guest room?"

She didn't say anything for a while. We walked down closer to the water. When we were up to our ankles, she stopped and played with the sand between her bare toes. "This might sound odd." She paused, sizing me up before continuing. "It's…You know, never mind." She dropped my hand.

"Come on. Tell me." We started walking again.

"No, it's weird."

"Okay, but if you get the urge." I held my arms out to say here I am.

"Thanks. Hey, you got another cigarette?"

"Yeah, they're in my backpack." I started to shrug the bag off my shoulders.

"Don't." Weston put her hand on the backpack. "I got it. Just tell me where they are."

"In the side pocket, the left side pocket." She unzipped the pocket and fished around until she pulled out a pack of cigarettes. "There should be a lighter in there too." I started to turn around to find the lighter.

"I got it. Stop twitching." Her hand pressed into my ribs to keep me from turning. It worked. I went really still. Even though there were a couple layers of clothing between us, my head went light and my heart sped up. The hand left my side, and the sound of the zipper brought me back from the little side trip my imagination went on. She handed me a lit cigarette.

"Thanks." Mmm, Weston cooties.

"So did you check out the eggs at the farmer's market?" She was teasing me. I was pretty sure.

"Yep, they were pretty much sold out."

"Did you really?"

"Yes. You told me to so I dragged Lauren and Ollie all the way to the very end to find out that there weren't any left. That place is intense, by the way." It was. The market went on for blocks, and you could do anything from buying produce that had been picked that morning to joining PFLAG or testing your Bible knowledge. And, yes, the PFLAG booth was right next to the Bible-thumpers. The market organizers had a sense of humor.

"I guess it was your first time there."

"Yeah."

"Aww, how cute. A Thursday Night virgin." She nudged me with her shoulder. My face started to burn from blushing. Awkward.

"I guess so. Someone could have warned me that it wasn't some pansy ass farmers market."

"First one in California."

"For real?" She nodded. "That's cool. Ollie and Lauren never know that kind of shit."

We continued down the beach talking. She told me about an art show she was doing. I told her why I hated San Francisco.

I didn't even notice how far we were walking so I was surprised when Weston stopped.

"Oh shit." Her eyes locked on to something over my shoulder.

"What?" I looked behind me. Nothing was there except a big rock about a mile away. It was a huge rock, actually, like half a mile wide huge. "Wait, is that Morro Rock?"

"Yep, we're almost in Morro Bay."

"Shit. How far did we walk?"

"Maybe five or six miles." She was still turning in circles. "I've never walked down this far. Fuck, what time is it?" She patted her pockets, but came up empty. "Can I use your cell phone?"

"Sure." My phone was somewhere in my backpack. I dug around until I found it at the bottom. "Here."

"Thanks." She dialed and waited. Trevor must not have picked up her home phone because she said, "Fuck. Fucking Trevor," then dialed another number. "Where are you?" There was a pause. "You can't just do that, Trev. I flipped." Another pause. "I took a walk on the beach and I didn't pay attention. I'm in Morro." She was yelling at him. I didn't get what she was mad at him for. That was between them, though. "No, you can't just..." I could hear him laughing. "Fuck off, Trevor." Less laughing. "No, you're right. Sorry. That's fine. Bye." She shut the phone shut with an angry little click.

"Problems?"

"No, just Trevor. He's being an ass. Actually, he isn't; I am. Well, he is a little."

A smile started across my lips. I tried to stop it; I really did.

"Oh God. I sound like I'm crazy."

"No, no. Perfectly sane." The smile was almost under control. Her eyes caught mine and we both started laughing again.

On the way back, it seemed like her shoulder touched mine more than necessary. Every time it happened it felt like electric currents were running through my body. That felt good. When she got close her leg would brush against mine. When we finally reached her house, we stopped in the sand looking up at it.

"So I guess I'll see you around." She looked disappointed. I knew I was.

"Definitely." I realized I really wanted her to stay. Or something. Maybe I just didn't want to leave.

"Cool."

"Hey, umm"—deep breath—"you want to go out sometime? Like to dinner?" Why did I ask that?

She didn't say anything and her face went blank. "I can't."

"That's cool."

"No, I wish I could, but I can't exactly date right now." She smiled to make it hurt less and placed her hand on my arm lightly.

"Don't worry about it. I just thought I'd give it a shot." I smiled. I did my best for one of those charming, I'm-so-hot smiles that usually made girls say yes. Why was I trying so hard?

"Listen, I'll probably be at Lucy's later. Maybe I'll see you there?"

"Totally."

Then she smiled. She was way better at it. That one dimple killed me.

Chapter Four

I started working normal people hours, like nine to five. It was weird because I was getting used to the whole getting up at dawn thing. It was almost becoming a habit. I could skate down to get coffee and hang out until the inevitable obnoxious phone call from Ollie. I seriously needed to make her change my ringtone back to normal. I was going down Ocean when it rang and scared the hell out of me.

"Dude, you have to change my phone back. I almost fell off my skateboard that time."

"Damn, you're already on your way."

"Lovely way to say hello, Ollie. I missed you too."

"Well, if you want to come over here for the interview that just called to cancel, that's fine by me."

"Are you kidding me? Kids these days, huh?" Whatever. It was my only interview that day so it was cool.

"That one looked older than you when she dropped off her app."

"See, the kids are the responsible ones. Very screwy world."

"Are you on something? You sound chipper."

"I think the ocean air is getting to me." I stopped my board so I could walk up the sidewalk without taking out any old ladies. "I'm almost at Lucy's. Want to meet me?"

"I do, but I'm just leaving for SLO."

"You suck."

"I know. Call me later."

"Sure." I hung up just as I reached the door to the coffee shop. Only two people were in line. I did a double take when I realized the second was Weston. Instead of the jeans I was used to, she was wearing a pair of tight board shorts that came to mid thigh and a white T-shirt. The shirt was almost transparent and the bathing suit top she had underneath was totally visible. I tried to keep from salivating.

"Cute outfit."

She turned at the sound of my voice and indulged me with a slow smile. "Shut up. I'm going surfing." That explained why she was built.

"I thought you had to do that at like five in the morning," I said oozing something other than intelligence.

"No." She laughed. "Sorry, you don't know much about surfing, do you?" I shook my head. "It depends on the tide, and that changes daily."

"Oh. How do you know when it'll be?"

"You gotta get a tide book." She pointed to a stack of little yellow books by the tip jar. Just about every business around town had a stack by the register. She grabbed one and flipped through. "See? Tide's perfect at eight forty-seven this morning so I have like an hour." She pointed at one of the many columns filled with numbers on the tiny page.

I tried to read, but it was already complicated and her hair kept brushing against my shoulder. The smell of her sunscreen reached me as she leaned closer to show the proper date and time. I decided to take her word for it because my vision was a little blurry.

"How about you? Working?" she asked before tossing the tide book back on the counter.

"I was, but my only interview just canceled." I grimaced. "So where are you surfing?"

"You know the beach off Studio at the end of town? It's decent."

"Aren't the waves huge down there?"

"No, they're only like five feet." My eyes must have gotten big or something because she started laughing again. "Don't you ever go in the ocean?"

"No way, man. In the Bay there are great whites." I shook my head emphatically. "Fuck that."

She looked at me weird. "But you can swim, right?" At my nod she continued, "And you've gone swimming in the ocean?"

"Of course."

The person ahead of us left and we stepped up to the counter. Weston looked back and forth between the barista and me like she was contemplating something. Finally, she focused her attention on the kid behind the counter.

"Hey, Jamie."

"'Sup, Wes. Surfin'?"

"Yep, make it two." Weston tossed a card on the counter.

"Want anything?" Jamie asked me.

"Yeah, I'll have my—"

"She's having the second one." Weston cut me off.

"Right." Jamie raised an eyebrow at me and walked away from the counter.

"Umm, what am I drinking?" I turned back to Wes.

"Soy milk, orange juice, and vanilla blended with ice. It's my pre-surf meal."

"Why am I having one?"

"Because you're getting a private surf lesson." Her gaze was on the movement behind the counter.

"Huh?" She had to be kidding.

Jamie set the drinks on the counter and swiped Weston's card. "Be nice to her, Wes. Nobody likes that 'wet suits are for wimps' lecture you give to first-timers."

"Very funny. I only did that once." Weston couldn't help smiling as she took back her card and handed me one of the drinks.

"But you guys did it to me!" Jamie looked at me. "Believe me, you want a wet suit."

"Trevor and I taught Jamie how to surf when she moved here," Weston explained.

I nodded. It was like I was watching a practiced scene, but no one had let me in on the joke.

"We'd better go if we want to make the tide. Come on." Weston headed for the door.

I followed, drink in hand. "Wait, you're serious?"

"Trevor will hook you up with a wet suit and a board."

I paused on the sidewalk and watched her walk away. I was starting to think she was serious.

Weston turned on the sidewalk. "Are you coming?"

My legs finally kicked in and I caught up with her. "Yeah." I tried a sip of the blended concoction. "Hey, this stuff isn't bad."

"I know." She smiled.

I followed her to the small surf shop on the corner. The flag above the door said Cayucos Surf Co. The interior was rough wood and smelled like new clothes and surf wax. There was a short flight of stairs at the back of the shop. We descended into the rental portion of the store.

"Tre-vor," Weston yelled.

"Wes-ton," returned a voice from the storeroom. A head appeared above the pile of boxes. "I'm coming out. Just a sec." He climbed over the boxes less than gracefully and tumbled into the room.

"Trev, this is Alden. Alden, Trevor." I looked him up and down as we shook hands. Dark hair that was in need of a cut hung over his eyes, his skin had a super deep tan, and he was built like Wes, but more. He was wearing a dark blue, long sleeve T-shirt with Rip Curl written down the sleeve and a pair of blue and green plaid shorty shorts.

"So you're Alden." He grinned ear to ear. Weston gave him a look that would reduce a child to tears, but he just kept smiling.

"Alden needs a suit and a board and we only have like fifteen minutes. Can you handle it or should we go over to Good Clean Fun?" Weston taunted him with the name of a rival surf shop.

"Tricks and posers, dude. They're tricks and posers." He clutched his heart and stumbled backward into the storeroom collapsing on some of the boxes. It didn't take him long to recover. He grabbed two wet suits from the line hanging in the storeroom. "I'll pull down a board for you. Heads, Wes." He tossed the wet suits to her and went outside through a side door.

"Turn around so we can see which one fits," Weston said. I complied and she held a wet suit against my back. Her hands closed over my shoulders holding the suit in place. They felt like fire burning through my T-shirt into my skin. She swapped the wet suits and, satisfied, hung one of them back up.

"You know she usually charges like twenty an hour for lessons," Trevor said from behind us. "Or she makes you pay in sexual favors." He started giggling at his own joke.

Wes looked ready to deck him. "Fuck off, Trev."

"Never. You'll never get rid of me."

"It's true." She glanced at me. "I keep trying to kill him, but he won't die."

"Never," Trevor repeated.

"So you ready to hit the waves?" She apparently decided to ignore him.

I realized I'd overlooked a rather important detail. "Umm, do I need a swimsuit? 'Cause I don't think I own one."

Wes laughed. "You live at the beach now, so it's about time. Go upstairs and pick one out." I did as I was told and tried not to think about her skin against mine. Or that she had no idea about the effect she was having on me.

Ten minutes later, we were on the beach clothed in neoprene with a ten-foot surfboard between us in the sand. We'd opted for the beach below the pier rather than the big boy waves down Highway One. Wes explained that this area was better for lessons.

"We're going to practice popping up here because in the water you'll have the weight of the wave pushing down on you and I want you to be used to it."

"Gotcha." I watched her lie down on the board to demonstrate. The back of her wet suit was still open, as was mine. A strip of tan skin and the blue string from her bikini was visible. The sight made my mouth dry and my wet suit feel very warm.

"You're going to do a fast push-up and use the momentum to jump to your feet. Like this." She braced her hands next to her shoulders, pushed up hard, and landed on her feet. Her feet were spread wide like she was on a skateboard. "It is harder than it looks so you can just go to your knees if you want. Like this." She repeated the process, but instead of standing, kneeled on the board. "Or you can use a knee up." This time she did a push-up to one knee and stood.

"All right, let me try."

She stepped off the board grinning. "Good luck."

I stretched out on the board and placed my hands the way Weston had. I did possibly the least graceful push-up ever and barely was able to get my knee under me. Wes started laughing, which made me laugh.

"You knew that was going to happen, didn't you."

"Totally." She gasped. "You just seemed so confident though. It was adorable."

"Great. I've always wanted to be adorable."

"Don't worry. Everyone does it their first time. Try again but use your knee to stand up." I did as instructed, and about five minutes later, I got my feet under me without the assistance of my knees.

"Am I like a pro surfer now?"

"Just 'cause you look hot in a wet suit does not mean you're a pro."

"I look hot in a wet suit?"

"You look hot in everything," she said with detachment. Hands down, best day ever. "Now try popping up again." I stretched out on the board again prepared to pop up. "But this time keep in mind that the waves are going to push down on you. Like this." She placed her palm on my back. "Pop up." I tried to move. The purpose of the exercise I'm sure was to demonstrate the weight of the water, but it was her touch that immobilized me.

"I can't."

"Sure you can. Just concentrate." She resituated her hand and shifted to the side so that I would have more room to move, but continued to press down. No swell could match the heaviness of her fingertips on my spine. With the soft touch gone, I was able to repeat the movement and land on my feet.

"That was awesome. Remember to land with your feet a bit wider. And use your hands to balance." She planted her feet in the sand and held her hands out palm down to demonstrate.

"Like this?" I mimicked her stance in the center of the board.

"Yeah, but you want to be back farther." I backed up a few steps. "A little more." She stepped on the board facing me. Her hands went to my hips and she walked me backward. I lost all my concentration and my stance. "Here." She stepped forward with her left foot forcing my right leg back into position. Only six inches of air separated us, and I could smell her sunscreen again. Her hands grasped mine, palm to palm, and lifted them lightly into place. "Good." Her breath whispered across my cheek when she spoke. Abruptly, she stepped back onto the sand and looked out at the ocean before I could decipher the look in her eyes. For a moment I could have sworn she was thinking the same thing I was.

"Should we get in the water?" I struggled back to normal ground.

"Yes, good idea. Here. Put the leash on." She tossed the leash to me and I sat on the board to secure it around my ankle. While I was occupied, Wes grabbed the long end of the zipper on her wet suit and pulled it up. Once connected to the surfboard, I did the same. It looked easier than it was. Wes lifted the front of the board without making eye contact. I picked up the back end and followed her into the water. It was fucking cold on my bare feet. The water swirled around us and took its time seeping into my wet suit.

I was already freaking out. I'm totally afraid of the ocean. Scenes from *Jaws* revisit me every time I'm up to my waist in water. I could see the kelp lolling around in the surf, which turned the water white and brown. It looked like a living thing with a parasite pushing to get out.

"Fucking freezing."

"Try not to think about it." She halted and looked back at me. "It isn't bad once you're in." The board was now floating in the water, but we each kept a hand on it until the water reached our thighs. "You're in charge of the board now. When you hit a wave, dip the nose down under it. You should go under now so the water won't shock you."

"Okay, sure." I ducked under a wave and opened my eyes under the brown water. Jaws was coming any second. The salt water burned my eyes and cold water slid the rest of the way into my suit through the neck opening. I watched Weston do the same thing next to me. We both stood. Her hair was long enough to stay pushed back, but mine suctioned to my forehead and more water poured into my eyes.

I waited for the next wave to get closer then jumped on the board and pushed the nose down. Miraculously, I came up on the other side. Wes was waiting up ahead for me. She was still able to stand, but when building waves passed her before their breaking point, she half-jumped, half-floated, and only her head was visible above the water. When I reached her she helped me turn the board.

"I'll tell you when to paddle. Remember, you should always look behind you so a wave doesn't surprise you."

"Will you be all right without a board?"

She looked at me with mock offense. "Hey, I was a lifeguard here every summer since I was sixteen. I think I can handle it." Her gaze returned to the ocean behind us. "There's a good one coming. You ready?"

"Hella."

"Wait for it." She jumped as another swell passed. "Look toward shore." She was still watching the wave. "Paddle, paddle, paddle."

I started paddling like nothing else, but my board stayed stationary. I looked back and Wes was holding me in place.

"Paddle, look to the shore." The breaker came within five feet of us. Wes gave the board a huge push. I was propelled forward and I felt the wave catch me. Suddenly, I wasn't in control of my own movement. It was the most bizarre and liberating feeling to have my power taken from me and by something inanimate no less. I just decided to trust it instead of fight it.

"Stand up. Stand up," Weston screamed from behind me. I placed my hands and pushed up hard. Wes was right; the water was heavy as hell and it shoved me down. The board wobbled while I was struggling to pop up. The nose dipped and I went under. Yum, salt water.

"Great job," Wes yelled as I started the trek back to her.

"Yeah, right," I screamed before ducking under a wave. Once I was in reach, she placed a hand on the board.

"That was awesome," she said as she held the surfboard steady for me.

"Whatever you say. I fucked it up." I smiled despite the fact that I blew it.

"No, you just had your weight too far forward. This time scoot back more when you paddle." A large swell was gathering behind us again. "You ready? This one is it."

"Gotcha." I tried to concentrate this time. The water started to move beneath me.

"Start paddling," Wes said. "Harder, paddle harder." I felt the wave carry me again and the push from Wes. "Go, go, go!"

I centered myself and gripped the sides of the board. I started to push up again and was able to pop into the air. The water tossed me sideways and my knees connected with the board by pure coincidence as I fell. The wave passed over my head, and I allowed the current to push me around until I could stand.

I wanted to keep an eye on the surf so I looked behind me immediately when I broke the surface. After the water drained out of my ears, I could hear Wes whooping at me. I pulled my board within reach again and swam to her. I tried a half a dozen more times, and each time the ocean kicked my ass royally, and each time I resurfaced, Weston cheered me on.

CHAPTER FIVE

When I finally landed on my feet, I lasted about half a second before the swell flicked me off the board. Wes was going crazy.

"You stood up!"

"Only for like a second." I tried to be modest.

"Doesn't matter. You totally stood up. You're awesome."

"I am pretty awesome." Modesty wasn't my nature.

"You're a genius at it then?" She jumped up and pushed me off the board. I fell backward in the water and came up sputtering.

"Ass." I was grinning so it wasn't very convincing.

"Unhook the leash. I'll show you how it's done." I handed her the end and she connected it to her own ankle. Wes straddled the board with her feet dangling in the water. She scooted back and forth finding her center of balance. The image gave me ideas that definitely did not involve surfing.

The wave grew behind her and she started paddling forward. She was way better at it than I was. When she paddled, there was actual movement. The board caught on the crest. Wes popped to her feet with no effort. She leaned in toward the wave, directing the board back and forth before diving into the water. When her head broke the froth, I started whooping in a damn good imitation of her. Thirty seconds later, she was back at my side.

"Pretty impressive."

"What can I say? I'm a pro," Wes said. "You think you can do it again?" She relinquished the board and handed me the leash. I climbed on and attached myself.

"Shouldn't you be able to do cooler tricks? Being a pro and all I mean."

"You want me to push you off?" She jumped and feigned like she was about to toss me on my ass. I flinched and held up my arms. "Naw, I wouldn't do that." At my look she started laughing again. "My board is like half this size. Shortboards are easier for tricks. Longboards are better for beginners."

"I'm not a beginner, I'll have you know. I can totally surf."

"All right, here's your chance, newbie. This wave is perfect."

I started paddling and waited for the push from the wave. The board was propelled toward shore and I immediately fell off. It took four more tries before I was able to stand again. When I finally did, I rode for a whole three seconds before falling off. Weston's cheers made people on the pier stare.

About half an hour later, we called it a day. I hadn't even thought about sharks most of the time we were in the water, so I thought I did pretty well. I was so tired by the time my feet hit dry sand that I didn't know if I'd make it up the beach.

"Dude, do you feel like you're dying?" I asked as we traipsed through the sand to the shower.

Wes just started laughing. Ahead of us, a father and his kids were rinsing off. That left Wes and me sharing a shower. We propped the board against the wall next to us and Wes turned on the spray. She left room for me. It wasn't a shower stall, just a pole with a couple showerheads. We had to stand very close to both to be in the water.

"Let me guess. You're thirsty as hell, your stomach is eating itself, you're freezing, and it feels like someone beat you up."

"That sounds about right." I watched her grab the zipper of her wet suit and tug it down. I tried to mimic the motion, but mine was stuck.

"Turn around." She unzipped me. "Wait until you're wearing warm clothes, you have food in your stomach, and you take a nap. It will be the best nap of your life."

She peeled her wet suit down as she spoke. I decided said nap would be much more enjoyable with a naked Weston. She held her now inside-out wet suit up in the spray until it was relatively free of sand. The wet board shorts she was wearing suctioned to her legs, outlining them. Her bikini top was absurdly tiny. For the first time I could see the muscles in her stomach and arms. It was a good thing I was already dripping water because I was getting wet just watching her. I concentrated on stripping off my wet suit and rinsing it like she had.

"Hand me your wet suit when you're done rinsing it out." She tossed her own over her arm.

"I think I'm done." I handed the suit to her.

Wes walked to her car about twenty feet from the shower and spread the suits over the low wall between the parking lot and the beach.

"You seriously wiped out on that last one," Wes said as she joined me again.

"Thanks for reminding me." I'd ridden too far in, so when I fell, the ocean floor welcomed me. My neck felt raw from where my head had dragged across the sand.

"You have sand everywhere." She reached up and ran her fingers through my hair. Her approach was purely clinical, just trying to get the sand out. Didn't matter her intention because it sure as hell felt good. "It looks like you brought half the beach with you." Her thumb moved behind my ear and rubbed until the sand caked on my skin rinsed away. My spine tingled. I loved it when she touched me.

"Thanks, Mom." Funny seemed the best approach. The other option was not allowed, especially on a public beach.

"Shit, your neck is all red. Does it hurt?" She made me turn and pushed my head forward so she could look at it.

"Not too bad." It just felt like a rug burn, a rug burn with sand and salt water in it.

"I can't see. You're too tall. Come here." Her hand closed around my wrist and she dragged me to where our wet suits were drying. "Sit." She pushed me down and tilted my head forward again.

"Wes, I'm fine. It's just raw. It doesn't even hurt." The tips of her fingers lightly rubbed it as if she could heal me with her touch.

"It looks okay. I just wanted to make sure." Her face was still bent close to me.

"So you think I'll pull through?"

So quickly I thought I imagined it, her lips brushed over the offending area. Fuck.

"There. Now you'll be fine." She said it like she'd put a Band-Aid on my neck rather than kissed it.

"Umm, thanks?"

"Whatever, asshole. I was trying to help." Playfully, she shoved me. "You want a towel?"

"Sure." I stepped over the wall and followed to her car. "And thank you. You practically saved my life." My tone was appropriately reverent.

"I knew you were an ass." But she was grinning as she tossed me a towel.

"Thanks." I dried my hair then hung the towel around my shoulders. "So you think I could interest you in some food?"

She studied my face for a moment. "That sounds like a good idea. What'd you have in mind?"

"I don't know. Why don't you pick? What's good? Is there some sort of after-surfing thing you're supposed to do?" I was definitely rambling, but she hadn't responded so it was making me a little nervous.

"How 'bout Duckie's?" She smiled finally. Why the hell do chicks do that? Just let you talk and make an ass of yourself.

"Awesome."

"I have pants if you don't want to wear your shorts. Nothing exciting, just sweats."

"Works for me."

Wes handed me my clothes and a pair of sweatpants. I watched as she managed to change out of her wet clothes while holding a towel around herself. One by one, the pieces of her bikini and her wet shorts dropped to the pavement. The entire process took about a minute and a half. I was impressed as hell. Sure, I was praying the whole time that the towel would lose just a little bit of altitude, but she had skill. It took me ten minutes to accomplish the same task. Once I had my boxers and a T-shirt on, I lost the towel. As I was pulling on sweats, I noticed that Wes was standing really still, like she was watching something. When I looked up her eyes cut back to the ocean. They totally reflected the color of the water. There was something deeper though. The teal of her eyes was pure where the ocean was diluted somehow.

"You ready to go?" she asked as I pulled my sweatshirt over my head.

"Sure." I grabbed my wallet and followed her. She stopped not even a hundred feet away by a little take-out window.

"Seriously? Right here?"

"Totally." She grinned. "Why do you think we eat here after surfing? You can order even if you're still wearing a wet suit and you can eat on the beach."

I just laughed.

"What do you want?" Wes was standing at the window already like she knew what she was getting.

"No, no. I want the whole experience. I'm guessing you get the same thing every time."

"All right." She smiled and turned to the kid waiting at the window. "Two clam chowders, two fries, and two waters." Her hand drifted to her pocket for her wallet so I stepped forward.

"I got it. It was my idea, remember?" At her nod I handed some cash through the window.

Right behind Duckie's was the smallest skate park I'd ever seen. It mostly consisted of a half-pipe and a couple rails. While we waited for our food we watched the kids skate.

"I didn't know there was a skate park over here."

"Serious?" Locals are always surprised when people are ignorant about their town.

"I guess I just never noticed. I'll have to try it out." I was already scoping the various angles.

"You any good?" Her shoulder bumped against mine.

"As long as I don't run into any pretty girls." That got her to smile. "You skate?"

"Nope, I'm terrible."

We fell into silence again watching the skaters until my name was called. I retrieved the food and followed Wes back to the low wall on the beach. There were benches on the sand just below the wall, but apparently it wasn't cool to sit there. The thing to do was to sit on the wall with your feet on the bench. She handed me two paper containers and a bottle of water. I drained about half the bottle in two seconds. Water was good. The clam chowder was pretty kickass too. In minutes, we'd both devoured our food.

We sat in silence for a while and just watched the ocean. It was a comfortable silence. Usually it takes me forever to enjoy sitting quietly with another human being. She was different.

People started slowly migrating onto the beach. The air was cold even though the sun was shining. Kids played in the surf oblivious to the temperature.

"So you and Trevor related?" I broke the silence.

"Me and Trev? No. Why?"

"Because you guys act like siblings."

She got quiet, thinking about what I said, I guess. "We kind of do, don't we?" I nodded. "I guess we sort of are. We grew up together 'cause our parents were friends. Like, we always went on vacation together and stuff." She shrugged.

"That's cool."

Wes nodded. "I guess. How about you? You grow up in San Francisco?" She studied me. Every time she touched me or looked at me, it seemed like I couldn't think or feel anything except for her.

"About an hour outside SF, but I moved there to work in a restaurant," I said when my synapses recovered.

"Miss it?"

"Not the city, no. I guess I miss my family." I shrugged. "Sort of. My older brother and sister live there. I mostly miss my niece and nephew. They're awesome." Then, for some reason, I told her what I rarely mentioned. "Thomas is technically my half brother. We all look identical though. Same boring brown hair and boring brown eyes."

Wes started laughing. "Boring?" I nodded. "I don't think there is anything boring about you. You're just…stunning."

I wasn't sure what to say to that. "Well, you're still out of my league."

"Shut up." She grinned.

"So how about you? Where's your family?"

She got still. Like really still. "My parents—" She stopped like she didn't know what came after that. "You know that morning we walked on the beach?"

"Uh-huh." I had no clue where this was going

"That was the second anniversary. Of their death," Wes clarified.

What the fuck? "Oh, man. I'm sorry, Wes."

She turned and smiled at me. "Thanks. But it's cool. I'm used to it by now. I don't know if that makes sense."

"Yeah, sure."

"Wow, that killed it, huh?"

"Nah," I lied. "I'm sorry, though." I was lacking as far as brilliant and sensitive responses went so I opted for stating the obvious. "I guess that's why you were on the beach at five in the morning." I wanted to ask what happened. Instead, I let her talk.

Wes grinned. "Yep. The beach always helps."

"I know what you mean. It's the same for me and skateboarding." I realized it wasn't exactly so I grimaced. "I'm really doing well with the whole sensitivity thing, huh?"

Weston laughed. "I think you're just what I need." I swallowed hard and gave myself a quick pep talk about meaning and intention. "How so?"

"Most people are all cautious, like I'll fall apart any moment."

"I doubt you will."

"Thanks." She smiled again. "So you miss you're niece and nephew, huh? You guys close?"

"Totally. They skate too, so I always take 'em out to the local park."

"You like kids?"

I didn't register the catch in her voice. "I guess. I like being an aunt 'cause when we're done skating I can just take them back to their parents, you know? I don't have to deal with bath time and feeding them and all that shit." I smiled at her, but she didn't smile back. Weird. Time for a subject change. "So are you totally beat from surfing?"

"Nope." She seemed to hesitate. "You have something in mind?"

"Want to walk the pier?" I wasn't ready to go away just yet. I wasn't ready to return to my normal boring life.

"I guess." We gathered the remains from our lunch and tossed it into the trash.

The pier was way too shady to go barefoot so we grabbed our shoes and started the trek down the worn wood. Unlike every other time I'd walked it, the pier was relatively empty. Only a few guys had fishing poles set up along the side. We leaned against the back of one of the newer, thus cleaner, benches at the end where, surprisingly, we were alone.

"I was out here a week or two ago and these guys hauled up an angel shark."

"Did they throw it back?" Wes was close enough that our hands were almost touching where they rested against the wood.

"No. They were dicks. When they brought it up they put a hole in its side. Then they just let it twitch."

"That's why I never use a gaff. A crab net works way better." She was as appalled as I'd been. "Anyway, if you're gonna keep something, you have to either kill it and clean it or put it in water."

"You fish out here?"

"Sometimes. Night fishing on the pier is a requirement in summer." She shrugged, which brushed her arm against mine.

"Sounds fun."

"It's cool." She looked over at me and grinned really big. "You still have sand in your hair."

"Nuh uh." I rubbed my hand through my nearly dry hair to get the sand out, but just ended up scraping the raw spot on my neck. "Shit, that stings."

"Stop it." Her hand enclosed mine and set it back on the bench. "I got it." She pushed off the bench and faced me.

My legs were stretched out and crossed in front of me so she had to straddle them. We were close enough that her inner thighs brushed against the outside of mine. She brushed her fingers through my hair right behind my ear. A shiver went through me. I tried not to let it show. It did. Her hand dropped, but she tilted her face up toward mine. With her sunglasses on I couldn't read her eyes. I brought my lips closer to hers anyway. She was inches away. Close enough so that I could feel her warm breath skittering across my lips. I wanted to kiss her. I had to. Right as I lowered my face, I heard footsteps coming up the pier. We both turned to watch a group of guys walk by us to the end of the pier where they started setting up their gear.

"I'm sorry," she said as she stepped back. "I should go."

"Don't."

"I have to. I'll see you later, Alden." And then she was walking back down the pier.

Fuck.

Chapter Six

I strutted up the walkway trying to remember everything I had to say. Weston's cleaned, borrowed sweats were folded under one arm. I knocked on the door with a bit more force than necessary. My stomach dropped when I heard footsteps approaching. I stared at my shoes hoping they might inspire confidence for a moment. When the door opened, my practiced speech died on my lips as I stared at the woman standing there. She was about ten years older than me. Her pale blond hair just brushed her shoulders and she was about a foot shorter than I was. She definitely answered the door like it was hers. Damn, must've gotten the wrong house. I could have sworn it was this one, but I'd only seen it from the beach side.

The woman's light voice interrupted my thoughts. "Can I help you?"

"I'm sorry I must have the wrong house." That's embarrassing.

"Who were you looking for? I know most of the neighbors." She seemed nice enough. It was worth a shot.

"Weston Duvall."

"You're in the right place."

"Oh, I…I'm Alden." I stumbled over my words. "Is, umm, she here?" Who the hell was this chick? Then it hit me. Weston had a girlfriend. Shit.

"Oh." A wide grin spread across her lips. "You're Alden. She's giving you surf lessons, right? I'm Anne." She extended her hand. I grasped it while Anne's words echoed through my head. Wes was giving me surf lessons. That was it. Suddenly, I had no idea why I was there. "Wes should be back soon. Why don't you come in?"

"No, it's cool. I'm sure I'll see her later." I had spent the last few weeks falling all over the girlfriend of the woman standing in front of me. I had no interest in hanging out with her. I backed away. I wanted to run, but knew I couldn't. "Here. I was just going to drop these off." I held out the sweatpants.

"Honestly, it's no problem. She'll want to see you and I could use the company." Anne stood aside and motioned me in. Seeing no way to politely refuse, I followed her through the house. She took the pants I was still holding and tossed them on a table by the door.

I glanced around. Most of the bottom floor was open. Everything was dark wood and glass like the exterior. The far wall was entirely windows that opened up to a small backyard, and beyond that the sea.

"So you and Weston own this place?" I wanted to know everything. Just so I could tell where the deceit was.

"No, no." Anne started laughing. "Something to drink?" She opened the fridge.

"Umm, just water." I felt like my tongue might fall out at any moment. It was dry and heavy, and it had nothing to do with the heat. Anne pulled two bottles of water from the fridge and handed one to me. "I thought Wes said she inherited it?"

She gave me a weird look. "Yes, her parents left it to her."

"But I thought you said—"

Anne cut me off. "Wes didn't tell you about me did she?" I shook my head. A smile crossed her face. "That explains a lot. I don't know what I'm going to do with her." She chuckled in a mom-like way. "I'm just here for Theo."

"Theo?" My confusion must have been apparent, but at that moment the sliding door opened and a little boy bolted into the room trailing sand and dripping water from his miniature wet suit. Even though his hair was soaking wet, I could tell it was the same as Weston's, honey-colored curls. It reached about an inch past his jaw and contained a copious amount of sand.

The kid's blue lips parted. "Trevor says I'm doin' way—"

His words vanished in Anne's command. "Stop right there. Don't even think about walking through the house like that."

"But I—" His small voice was lost again as she shooed him back outside.

"Sorry. Do you mind? We will just be a moment," Anne said as she stepped out the door.

I nodded, dumbfounded. Of all the things I expected to happen when I came, this was at the bottom of the list. Hell, it wasn't even on the list. How could Weston have a kid? It was good I was alone because my useless mouth was hanging wide open. I watched the pair of them walk to a shower behind the house. Anne helped Theo reclaim his limbs from the navy blue and neon yellow wet suit. She leaned over and turned on the shower, pointing at his feet. Once Theo was relatively sand free, Anne wrapped a gigantic towel around him and led him back inside. Theo's eyes got wide as he noticed me for the first time. A grin stretched across his tan, freckled face.

"Hi, I'm Theo."

"I'm Alden." I extended my hand to him. He placed his small hand in mine and shook it with great exaggeration. He looked about five. I did some math in my head. Weston must have been about eighteen when he was born. That didn't make any sense.

"I just got back from surfing," he proclaimed loudly. "Trevor says I'm his best student."

"That's great, T, but you need to put some dry clothes on," Anne said.

He made a dramatic pouting face and ran up the stairs.

"And brush your hair," she yelled after him.

I found my voice again, but was embarrassed when it cracked. "I didn't know Wes had a…had a kid."

Anne's brow wrinkled then her expression became unreadable. "I think Wes just pulled in. Maybe she should explain."

I nodded and we waited in silence until the door opened.

"Thanks for waiting, Anne. You're the best." Weston dropped her keys on the table just inside the door. Her camera and laptop bag were next. She was doing the twenty-something business look today. Dark gray pants and a button up shirt rolled to her elbows.

Her hair was straightened so it fell into her eyes. "Is Theo back? Did Trevor stop in? Did he say how…" She finally looked up and the rest of her sentence trailed away into, "Alden."

"Umm, hey."

"What are you doing here?"

Well, I was going to demand that you go out with me. But now that I've met your wife and child that would probably be inappropriate. "I just wanted to ask you something. But I should go." It sounded like a good idea, but she was between me and the door and it didn't look like she was moving.

"No, you shouldn't."

"I should." I edged past her, but she followed me outside.

"Alden, wait."

"What?" My senses were starting to come back. How could she not tell me about her little family?

"We should talk."

"What could we possibly have to talk about?"

She looked uncomfortable all of a sudden. It looked like it was sinking in for her too. "What did you come to talk to me about?"

"That? It's nothing." I tried to contain the acerbic tone, but it wasn't ready to be contained.

"Why?"

Because you have a wife and fucking kid, I wanted to scream. I settled for throwing my hand indignantly up toward the house.

"We can't talk anymore because of Theo? Kids scare you? Maybe this is why I didn't tell you about him." She looked a little pissed off now. I didn't see why she was mad. She wasn't the one being lied to.

"You didn't think it might be a good idea to tell me about your wife and kid? So that I could stop flirting with you and making an ass of myself." The anger and disappointment made every word rough so I had to force each one out of my throat. "Fuck, how old were you when he was born? Eighteen?"

"Seventeen." She started smiling. Not in a good way. She still looked furious, but the corners of her mouth twitched into a small humorless grin. "Do you ever wait for anything or do you always just fly off like that?" Definitely rhetorical so I kept my mouth shut. "I don't have a wife, or a girlfriend. I don't have a kid either. I have a little brother who came to live with me when our parents died. I also have a nanny to help take care of him." Shit, my bad. "I'm sorry you feel you have to run away now that you realize my roommate is a five-year-old."

"You think that's why I'm mad?" Even if she wasn't married, I was still pissed that she never mentioned the kid. Everything just got serious. And way the fuck out of my league.

"That's why most people freak out. Kids scare twenty-year-olds."

"Damn right they do." The tone finally dropped, making me sound like a child. "It would have been nice to know." I turned to leave, but she grabbed my arm stalling my forward motion.

"I'm sorry, Alden." She was begging without saying it.

I shrugged her hand off and walked away.

I was lying on my futon staring at the ceiling. I'd been too drunk the night before to pull it out, so my feet hung over the edge.

Ollie's solution had been to get trashed and roam the streets of San Luis. I didn't see why. My life had just gotten easier. Girls were too much trouble. That's why I didn't date much. Like everything else in life, the trouble wasn't worth it. I didn't like to work too hard, so I didn't. I didn't want a wife and kid, so I didn't have either. Everything could be answered by one simple question: Was it worth it? Most things weren't. Wes was now in that category.

So what if I was a dick for admitting what most people were afraid to say.

Taking half a bottle of aspirin and drinking my weight in water wasn't making the hangover go away. A shower sounded like a good idea, but that involved moving. Staying very still seemed the best option. A car pulled up in front of the house. I figured it was the people staying next door so I ignored it until there was a knock at my door. I reached for the remote and turned up Billie Holiday.

Maybe they would get the hint and go the fuck away. When the knock sounded for the third time, I went to answer it.

The door swung wide and I leaned against the frame. I let Wes look me up and down. Her gaze lingered on the worn basketball shorts that defied gravity by clinging below my hips. My nipples got hard from the way she was looking at me. When she saw the reaction through my thin T-shirt, she sucked her bottom lip between her teeth. My mouth went dry and other places went wet.

"What do you want, Wes?"

"Sorry. Were you asleep?" She looked at my hair. It was probably sticking out at weird angles. "I thought you'd be up. It's like eleven."

"Did you come here to lecture me? 'Cause I'd rather not do that." I moved to close the door, but stopped at her hand on my arm. The touch made me freeze.

"I came to apologize. You were right. I should have told you about Theo."

I left the door open and went to sit back down on the couch. Wes followed and sat next to me.

"I wanted to tell you, but I was afraid you'd react like this."

"React like what? We've talked so much. Don't you think you could have mentioned at some point, 'oh, by the way, I've got a kid?' Seems like something you might want to bring up in conversation." My voice was coming out a little high-pitched, and it kind of sounded like I was yelling. I leaned my head against the couch and closed my eyes. This was not helping the headache.

"I'm sorry. I don't know what to say."

"You know it doesn't matter," I said more to myself than to her. I rubbed my eyes and ran my hands through my hair. "I think you should go." I was doing my best not to look at her because I was pretty sure she could tell I was full of shit.

"No, you don't." Yep, she could tell. "And I'm not leaving until you talk to me."

I was torn. Part of me was pissed and the other part, well, Wes looked really hot. She had come straight from surfing because her hair was still wet and it had started to curl. Her dark blue polo was soaked through from the swimsuit underneath. Since I couldn't decide between kicking her out and fucking her blind, I compromised.

"Whatever. You can talk. I'm going to take a shower."

"Come on, Alden. Talk to me."

"Nope. I'm ignoring you right now."

"Mature."

Like I'd never heard that before. I shrugged and walked into the tiny bathroom. She followed and leaned against the door making it impossible to close. I'm sure her intention was to annoy me into talking, but her persistence was just turning me on more. Now instead of a steady throb in my head there was one between my legs. I'd just have to tell myself to forget she was watching. I hooked two fingers in the collar of my shirt and tugged it over my head. If not for her quickening breath, I wouldn't have known I was having any effect on her. We saw each other practically naked when we were surfing, I reasoned. It so wasn't the same. I leaned in and turned on the water.

It was time to call her bluff so I dropped my shorts and stepped into the spray. The glass door shut behind me. Not that it did much. The glass wasn't frosted so you couldn't help but see through the walls. I did my best to ignore her. I lathered my hair and put it in a Mohawk with the suds. When I sneaked a glance in her direction, she was staring at the doorframe and trying not to smile. The moisture soaking my thighs had nothing to do with the water and a lot to do with her concealed scrutiny.

Finally, I shut off the water and got out of the shower. I dried my hair then wrapped the towel around my waist. No, I didn't wear a towel like a girl. It looks stupid and I didn't have much in the way of tits. Wes shook her head and went back to the living room. I brushed my teeth, styled my hair, put on sunscreen, anything to make her wait.

When I sauntered out of the bathroom, she was leaning against the back of the futon. I opened the closet to dig around in my dresser. Billie Holiday was still playing, and it was more audible now. I began to mouth the words to "You're my Thrill." I didn't hear Wes come up behind me.

"What's your scar from?" she asked quietly.

"Which one?" I responded against my better judgment.

"This one." Weston traced a finger along the two-inch long ridge of scar tissue along my ribs.

"I fell off my skateboard and landed on a piece of glass." I tried to ignore the soft touch that shot straight down my spine melting everything in its path. The muscles in my face didn't seem to be listening when I told them to smile. She nodded and I continued talking, attempting to hide my arousal. "What about yours?" I pointed to her stomach where I knew there was a white abrasion along the crest of her hip.

"Surfing. I was in a rocky area and the rock won." She lifted the edge of her shirt showing a flat, tan stomach.

It seemed like I watched myself touch her from across the room. My hand moved across the gap between us and settled itself on her hip. Thumb pressed to the soft inner curve, fingers splayed on her side. Without realizing what I was doing, I pressed lightly, drawing a small moan from her. Our foreheads pressed together, lips inches apart.

"Please tell me you aren't mad anymore because—"

I kissed her so she would stop talking. It was her uncertainty that got me. Besides, if I waited any longer to touch her I thought something in me might die. Damn, her lips were soft. They tasted sweet and a little salty from the ocean. She didn't pull away. Instead, she kissed me so that I couldn't think or feel or hear anything. The fabric of her shirt was rough against my bare nipples. My left one was so sensitive from the ring through it that it was skirting the edge of pain. Fuck. I was so only wearing a towel and we hadn't even been on a date and she had a kid and I had no idea what I was doing.

"Wait. We should stop." It took all my strength to survive without kissing her because I knew that was where I belonged. But we had to do this right, which was probably not at all.

"You're right. I can't do this." That wasn't what she was supposed to say.

"You can't do what?" We were both breathing hard. My defenses were seriously damaged at the moment, and if she didn't explain herself soon I was going to just fall apart. Maybe fall down and die. My question hung between us and expanded until the distance hurt. I couldn't fill my lungs. Like I was drowning.

"I should go." She turned and walked toward the door.

"No. Wait. Don't." I followed her. For just a second, she looked at me. Her eyes were bruised and darker than I had ever seen them. "Just wait. Let me get dressed. We'll talk." I held up my hands in surrender. "Please."

The nod she gave was so slight that I felt rather than saw it. I dressed hurriedly. The first pair of jeans I saw and a T-shirt.

"Let me show you something." I didn't check to see if she was following. I just went out the door. I was careful on the firewood so I wouldn't get splinters in my feet. On the roof I turned and sat with my legs dangling over the edge. Wes climbed on the firewood and took the hand I offered. I pulled her up next to me. We stood using our held hands for balance. The best place to sit was facing west looking at the ocean. The sun was just starting to burn the morning fog, and we could barely see the pier and the oblivion of the bay giving way to open sea. For maybe ten minutes, we just sat. She didn't let go of my hand.

"I…" I didn't know what to say. Billie was still playing inside. "I can't get you out of my head, Wes. It's like when I'm around you I can do anything, be anything, because you think I can." The words started pouring out and I couldn't stop them. "Hell, I learned to surf because of you. I can't stand the ocean. I'm totally afraid of it, I can't swim, I hate kelp, and I'm afraid of sharks. I'll probably need years of therapy." That sounded obsessive. I needed more convincing, less I'm-stalking-you.

Wes started laughing. Not chuckling or anything, full on laughing. I didn't know if I should join her or just jump off the roof and get it over with. She was gasping for air now. I knew I wasn't that funny.

"I'm sorry. I don't know why I'm laughing." She laughed some more. "You think I fuck you up?" She was still grinning. Her one dimple was really pronounced. It was so sexy. "The amount of time I spend at Lucy's has tripled since I met you. Hell, I'm going through film like the first time I got a camera." The laughter stopped. "I was just hoping that maybe, just maybe, you would have something wrong with you so I could walk away. But I can't seem to walk away." Her tone was appreciative and frustrated. But then her smile dropped. "But I can't stay. I just can't." Okay, let's be positive; she likes me. It was like being in sixth grade and you just got the note back and they checked yes. Except more painful. Less fun too.

"Why?" I sounded a lot more together than I was.

"Theo."

"Come on, Wes. I like kids. You have to give me a chance. Give me something. We'll all go out, like the three of us." I must have been insane. I didn't know who I was trying to convince. Me or her. I just decided to roll with it.

"He's not just a kid you can give back when you're done having fun."

Shit. I might have deserved that one. "I know. But why not give it a shot?"

"And then what? In six months when you're bored of having a kid around or we're bored of each other? What do I tell him then?"

"I don't know." It was the truth.

She let go of my hand and stood. "I'm sorry." I tried to meet her eyes, but she looked away and climbed down. Hours passed while I sat on the roof. The sun finally burned away the mist covering Cayucos. I waited, hoping her touch would somehow seep out of my skin and evaporate into the warm salt air. It didn't.

Chapter Seven

Three days passed. Ollie got my coffee every morning so I didn't have to go into Lucy's. I spent my time in the kitchen cooking and working out our menu with Cliff. I kept drinking Red Bull and forgetting to eat.

None of it worked.

Ollie eventually forced me into her car and took me to San Luis. We went into Woodstock's where she ordered a huge pizza. I didn't realize I was hungry until I ate half of it.

"You want to talk about it?" She was only on her second piece.

"Not so much." Every item on the table needed rearranging. I diligently stepped up to the task.

"Alden." I glanced up. "Tell me. You'll feel better."

"I don't think I want to."

"How about I start you off?" I looked at her curiously. "Three days ago Weston showed up at Delma's asking where you were. I told her where you lived."

"I kissed her." My eyes dropped to the table again.

"What?" Her half-eaten pizza hit the plate.

"She came over to apologize, and I'm not sure what happened." I shrugged. "We ended up kind of making out and then she took off."

"That's good, right?" She started eating her pizza again.

"It could be better. She said she doesn't want to see me because of the kid."

"What do you mean?" Ollie finished her pizza and grabbed another slice.

"I might have, maybe, told her kids were fun as long as you can give them back to their parents when you get bored. Or something."

"Dumbass. What else?"

"I don't know. Something about how I'll get bored having a kid around or we'll break up and he will be devastated."

"But you love kids." She said it like it was pure logic.

"I don't think that's what it's about." She waited for an explanation. "When my mom started dating, it drove me and Katie and Thomas crazy. The guys we liked never stayed. The ones we hated would stick for years. You know?"

"No. I'm not following." Ollie grew up in a two-parent household where dinner was on the table at the same time every night, no questions asked.

"When you have a kid, whoever you date, they date. When you break up, they break up."

"So if Weston went out with you then the kid would be going out with you?" She said it slow like she was trying to keep up.

"Kind of. So I can see why she wouldn't do that to him." I hesitated. "And why I should leave them alone." I didn't need to tell her the last part. Ollie and I both knew the chances of me sticking around weren't great. I'd made a conscious decision to never grow up. That wasn't going to change.

"Why don't you just tell her you understand?"

"Because I don't. There's no way for me to get that. There's no way for anyone to know until it happens to them." I started talking faster and a bit louder.

"Hey." She kicked me under the table. "Shut up." Her eyes locked onto something behind me.

"What, dude?" I turned around and caught sight of Wes and Theo walking in. Both were clad in neon board shorts that came to knee level. Their hair matched too. Wes had hers in a ponytail, and Theo's was pulled away from his face on top with the back down.

"Damn," Ollie said. "They're pretty, aren't they?"

"What do I do?" I tried to turn back, but she had seen me. There was nothing to do except smile and wave. They came toward our table.

"Smile. And make eye contact. It makes you hotter."

"Hey, Wes." I smiled. Ollie told me to.

"Hey." Wes smiled too. Damn, she was good at that, smiling I mean. "This is Theo. I don't know if you guys properly met." She set her hand on his shoulder.

"Hi, Theo. I'm Olivia." Ollie shook his hand. She looked a little stunned. Maybe she was figuring out that he was real.

"Hello, Olivia." He smiled his sister's smile then looked at me. "I remember you. You're Alden." Every word he said was over enunciated like he was trying it for the first time.

"That's right." This was awkward.

"So what are you guys doing here?" I don't know why Ollie asked. It was pretty obvious.

"Just getting some dinner. It's Theo's night to pick." Wes and Ollie kept talking. I nodded along pretending I was following. I wasn't, until I heard my name.

"What?" Okay, I sounded like an idiot.

"I said we almost have a menu." Ollie was looking at me meaningfully, but I didn't get the meaning.

"Uh-huh. We just have to test it out." Why was she talking to them about the menu?

"So what are you two doing tomorrow night?" Ollie grinned at me and returned her attention to Wes and Theo. Then I realized what she was doing. What a bitch. I kicked her under the table. She kicked back.

"Not much." Wes shrugged and glanced at me, confused.

"Great. Then come by Delma's around seven. We're doing a trial run of the menu to narrow it down. Cliff and Alden are making tons of food. Cliff's bringing his wife and kids and my grandmother is coming, but we still need more guinea pigs. It'll be fun. I promise." Ollie was devious. We totally had enough people coming. I was going to kill her. I'd have to thank her first.

"You sure?" Wes looked at me.

Ollie kicked me again. My shins were going to bruise.

"Definitely. It'll be a good time."

"Plus, Alden is an amazing chef." Ollie dramatically closed her eyes and tipped her head back. "Amazing." Loser.

"All right. We'll be there."

"Wes." Theo spoke for the first time since he was introduced. "Weessss, I'm hungry." He started pulling on her hand.

"All right, little dude." Wes yanked him closer and pulled him in front of her. "But ask nice. Don't be rude." She settled her arms over his shoulders and crossed them over his chest. They looked natural and perfect with their exact features. Their eyes, mouths, even the freckles across their tan noses were the same.

"Sorry." He looked up at her.

"Don't tell me. Tell them."

"I'm sorry." He made eye contact with me then Ollie when he said it. This kid had better manners than me. Not that it was a challenge.

"We'd better get a table." Wes released Theo. "I guess we'll see you guys tomorrow."

"Later." I watched them walk away and snag a booth on the other end of the restaurant. "Ollie, what the hell are you doing?"

"Eating pizza." She had already turned back to her forgotten food.

"Hilarious. I mean inviting them."

"The longer someone hangs around you, the more they fall in love with you. So I'm creating an excuse for her to hang out with you." Ollie was in the habit of saying crazy things as if they were common sense. She had the perfect disinterested delivery.

"What?" Who said I wanted Wes to fall in love with me?

"I'm not going to repeat this. I don't want to inflate your ego. Listen closely." She took a swig of soda. "You are charming and totally hot. You are also an idiot, but you even make that seem sexy. You follow?"

"You're on crack."

"Believe me. Even Grandma has a crush on you. Ask her."

"Crack."

"Fine. Don't believe me. It's still true." She shrugged. "Want to get out of here?"

"Sure," I said as we stood. "And thanks. For inviting them."

"Just don't screw it up. I hate when you get depressed." She slid her arm around my waist. Automatically, I draped my arm over her shoulders.

"Whatever."

❖

Ollie had invited way more people than I thought. Apparently, she told Cliff instead of me. Ollie sucked. There was plenty of food, though. Delma, Ollie's grandma, got there before everyone and harassed the shit out of us. I guess she thought buying Ollie a restaurant justified being cruel. It sort of did. She also insisted that since she was paying me she could order me to hang out with her all night instead of working in the kitchen. When I insisted on doing my job, she threatened to fire me. As people arrived, Delma and Ollie and I greeted them. Lauren got there an hour in and stayed up front with them so I went back to the kitchen.

When Cliff's family showed up, I sent him out so he could give them the tour. After fifteen minutes, he came back in the kitchen and told me that Delma wanted me back. I gave him my most exasperated sigh, but he still pushed me into the lobby.

"There she is." Delma abandoned Ollie and Lauren at the door to grab my arm and drag me with her. "I can't be alone that long. What were you doing?"

"My job." I smiled.

"I thought I was going to fire you." She slid her arm through mine. At that moment the door opened admitting Wes and Theo. Wes looked around until her eyes locked onto my face. I stepped forward then stopped myself. She smiled. Theo immediately left Wes's side to shake Ollie's then Lauren's hand. Very sociable. Wes sauntered toward Delma and me.

"Hey, Alden."

"Wes." An elbow was pressed into my side. "Oh, Wes, this is Delma. She's Ollie's grandmother. And this is my friend Weston." Delma took Weston's hand and didn't show signs of letting go.

"Is this one of those times you say friend when you mean something else and I don't find out until two months later?" Delma asked mischievously. She was evil.

My jaw dropped. Literally. Wes looked straight up, shocked. "I'm sorry about her," I told Wes. "She's getting pretty senile. We're putting her in a home next week." Wes started grinning. At least she wasn't running the other direction.

Delma let go of Wes so she could slap my arm lightly. "You are not. I asked a simple question."

I hated when Delma teased me. She always chose the most unfortunate audience. "No, Delma, I said friend and I meant it." Wes was still standing there looking a little shell-shocked.

"Perhaps you should do something about that." Delma smacked my arm again. "She is absolutely beautiful."

"Delma!"

"Thank you," Wes finally chimed in. Anything to get the old lady to stop talking I guess.

"You're welcome."

"It doesn't matter anyway," I told Delma. "I tried, but when I asked she said no."

Delma's eyes got big. "Why? You two would look wonderful together." Delma pushed me until I was standing next to Wes, then she linked our arms together. I was pretty sure I was going to die of embarrassment at any moment. "Look at you."

That was when Theo walked up.

"Hi, I'm Theo." He extended his little hand to Delma.

"Hello, Theo. I'm Delma." She shook his hand.

"This is my brother." Wes let go of my arm to set a hand on Theo's shoulder.

"I can see that. You are very handsome," Delma told Theo.

"I look like Wes." You can always tell when a kid is repeating something they've heard.

"You certainly do. Will you be my escort?" Delma was smitten.

"What's a escort?"

"It means you will walk around with me and say hello to people."

"Okay." Theo shrugged. He was easygoing.

"I thought I was your escort." I wasn't offended. It made my night a hell of a lot easier.

"You're a slouch. And I believe that you will be keeping Weston company. Will you not?" Was it that obvious?

"I'm not sure I want a slouch hanging around me." Oh, now Wes was going to be funny.

"Too bad. You're stuck with me," I shot back. "That's what Delma wants." Wes just shook her head and took my hand.

"You better give me the tour then."

"If that's what you want."

"Oh, no, it's what Delma wants." Hilarious.

Chapter Eight

I was running the kitchen. It was my job, after all. The night was coming to a close finally. We were finishing the preparations for dessert when Wes and Theo came down the stairs loudly.

"Weessss. I don't wanna."

"Sit." Wes pointed to a chair and Theo slumped into it.

"I don't like 'em," Theo said to his sneakers.

"I know. But if you want dessert you have to." I knew this talk. It was a nightly occurrence with my niece.

"They're gross."

I signaled Cliff and got him to take over for me. Wes was kneeling in front of Theo.

"Hey, guys. What's up?"

"I'm not doing it." Theo had his hands curled around the edge of his seat.

"Vegetables," Wes offered in explanation.

"I figured. Hey, Theo." He looked up at me. "You like pizza?" He nodded slowly. "If I made you one where you couldn't taste the vegetables would you try it?"

"What kind?"

"What do you like on pizza?"

"Pepperoni and sausage."

"All right then, pepperoni and sausage."

"I'll try it." He was banking on try, no commitments.

"Cool. You wanna watch me make it?" I indicated the tall chairs at the counter facing into the kitchen.

"Yeah." That brought out a bit of excitement. He scrambled up a chair forcing Wes to jump forward to make sure he didn't fall. She looked back at me and mouthed thank you.

"All right, Theo. You can park it on the counter, but don't lean into the kitchen." He sat on the counter. "See the stove here?" At his nod I continued. "When I'm cooking, it can be dangerous because of the fire."

"Cool." Yep, I was impressive.

"So you want to know what I'm doing?"

"Yeah."

"All right. I'm pouring olive oil in this pan." I grabbed the bottle and poured it from about a foot above the pan then pulled it up while tapering off the stream. I was showing off a little. "Now garlic." I tossed in minced garlic. "And this is rocket." I held up a handful of greens.

"Rocket? Like a spaceship?"

"Exactly." He didn't need the other names. Arugula sounded so boring. "And some spinach and basil." I added a few more leaves to my cutting board and started chopping. When my oil was ready, I threw in the chopped green stuff. "Now sit back."

"Why?" He was already leaning way too close.

"Because I'm going to toss it." Wes pulled him back by his waistband. Tossing shit in the air is one of those things that looks fucking cool, is easy to do, and never smart if you don't know what you're doing. Whatever. With a twitch of my wrist, I threw the pan forward then up, forcing the contents to do a perfect little twist out of the pan then back in. A couple more times and I got decent height. I knew what I was doing.

"Cool." Theo's eyes got wide.

"Now we need sauce." I turned off the heat and disappeared into the fridge. I returned with a ball of dough and small bowl of sauce. I left the oil in the pan and stirred the wilted greens into the sauce. If I added them on top of the pizza the way it was supposed to be done, Theo would be able to pick them off. In the sauce, he'd never notice. I'm tricky.

I kneaded the dough then started stretching it over the backs of my fingers. I gave the round a couple tosses in the air for good measure.

"What's that?" he asked as I set what looked like a wooden paddle on the counter.

"A pizza peel. You make the pizza on it then use this handle to put it in the oven."

I glanced up and realized Wes was studying every movement. That was weird. It made my stomach do somersaults. My hands started to shake slightly as I spread sauce over the dough. I got it under control for the toppings. Concentrate. I just had to focus on what I was doing. Spreading chunks of salami, crumbed linguica, olives, and finely sliced mushrooms over the thin layer of cheese. Theo asked what each topping was and I would give him a bite to try.

Once the pizza was finished I let it cool slightly, cut it a couple times through the center with a flourish, and slid it on a plate in front of Theo.

"Thanks." He vibrated in his seat. "Can I try it now?"

"Sure, but it's hot. Be careful."

Hesitantly, he picked up a piece and took a bite. After chewing for a second, he grinned. "Tastes like pizza."

"You like it?"

He nodded vigorously, unable to talk due to a mouthful of cheese and salami. The pizza was a good ten inches across, just larger than a personal pizza. Theo put away about a third of it. That was a lot for a little kid.

"Wes, I'm full."

"Not too full for dessert, right?" she said.

"No." He looked sick and excited at the thought.

"We just sent it upstairs. If you want some you better be quick," I told him.

"Okay." Theo jumped out of his seat. "Come on, Wes." He pulled at her hand.

"Theo." Wes had that tone down. The one that says you're forgetting something and you're in trouble.

"Oh, yeah. Thanks for making me pizza, Alden." He smiled big. "Now can we have dessert?"

"Sure." Wes let him pull her a bit closer to the stairs. "Thanks, Alden." She stopped to reach back and squeeze my hand then allowed Theo to continue dragging her.

❖

"Will someone get that?" Even from the kitchen I could hear the pounding on the back door. We were pretty much done cleaning. There were just a couple guys left helping me close up. I'd sent Cliff home with his family and Ollie had taken Lauren and Delma home.

"I think it's for you," someone called back. Light from the parking lot painted the floor so I knew the door was still open. No one came in.

"I'll be right there." I skirted around the poor kid who'd gotten stuck mopping and replacing the floor mats. Finally, I was able to walk through the dark dining room to the back door. Wes was leaning against the frame. "Hey."

"Hey. Are you guys still busy?" She nodded in the direction of the kitchen.

"No, no. Just finishing up."

"Cool." We both nodded. Yep, it was cool.

"So uhh…what are you doing here?"

"I'm not sure."

"You want to come in?" I held the door open.

"Sure." She stayed close on my heels until I reached the kitchen. "Should I just wait out here?"

"Go ahead and snag a table. I'm going to change." I indicated the kitchen clothes I was wearing.

"Right. Okay." She sat on the edge of a chair. It looked like she was ready to bolt any minute.

I let everyone know they could take off then went to change. I ditched my stark white chef's jacket and baggy black pants and pulled on my jeans and Vans. Then I ditched the tank top I wore under my jacket and pulled on a button up shirt. On my way out of the kitchen I hit all the lights downstairs. Light from the street came in through the windows. It was enough to offer her my hand and lead her up the stairs.

"You want something to drink?" I moved around the counter to play bartender. "I'm gonna have a Corona."

"That sounds good."

Upstairs was dark too. I flicked on one of the lights so I could cut a couple lime wedges without losing a finger. I placed a piece of fruit in each of the open bottles I'd set on the bar.

"Here." I pushed the drink toward her. Then I turned off the light and grabbed my beer so we could walk outside. We leaned against the railing looking at the dark beach that was only feet away

"Thanks for earlier," Wes said without looking at me.

"What do you mean?" I hadn't invited her. That was all Ollie.

"For getting Theo to eat his vegetables. You were very suave." She set her beer on the railing and slowly pushed the lime into the bottle. Lime juice squirted onto her finger and she absentmindedly licked it off. The slow dip of her finger into her mouth made me ache.

"It wasn't a big deal," I managed to respond.

"It was." I nodded along. If she thought it mattered, then it mattered. "I'm not sure why I'm here," she repeated. "You probably want to go home."

"No, I don't." There was no point in lying.

"But Olivia's grandmother is in town and so is your friend." She did the thing where she emphasized the word friend again.

"Do you not like Lauren?" Might as well get it out there.

"What?" For a second I thought she was going to choke on her beer. "Why? What do you mean?"

"I don't know. You just seem weird around her. I got the impression that you're not a fan." I was pretty sure she assumed the same thing everyone assumed.

"No. I've got no problem with her." At least she managed a little sincerity.

"You're not jealous of her are you?" I shifted to watch her expression.

That time she did choke. She set the bottle down with a thud and worked on swallowing. Her recovery was quick. She went from choking to ice queen in two seconds flat. "Why would I be jealous?" she asked calmly. I half smiled and pointed to myself. "Oh, get over yourself." She twisted to look at me. With her that close, I could smell her hair. It was like oranges and something else. "It is a little weird that she calls you doll face."

"I know. I hate it." I shrugged. "But it's not my fault I'm so hot." I wasn't.

"No, it's not." She didn't seem to be kidding. Her fingertips touched my cheek lightly. Like she was checking if I was really there. Then she kissed me. Instinctively, I cupped her face in my palm, drawing her in. I wasn't letting go. Not like before. Her tongue pushed insistently against my mouth. I allowed her in just to fight back. We nearly fell over in our need to be closer even though our bodies were already pressed together. She backed against the railing and spread her legs enough for me to stand between them. My hips seemed to grind into her of their own accord. She sucked my bottom lip then bit hard enough to draw blood.

Fuck, I was going to die if I didn't have her right there. I finally slid a hand beneath her shirt. The material rose, exposing her stomach. When I felt the bare skin pressed into mine, I glanced down to see her unbuttoning my shirt with one hand while her other twisted into my hair. She tipped her head back giving me her neck. When I ran my tongue along her exposed skin, she jerked a little. Then she tugged me closer by my hair. That was fucking hot. The movement made the railing behind her shake. Glass shattered on the pavement below. We ignored it. Then it happened again.

"Fuck," I said. She started laughing. "What?"

"Did we just lose the beer?"

"Yep." Damn.

"That killed it didn't it?"

"Yep," I murmured. "Fuck."

She pushed me back just a little. Her lips met mine again, but it felt different. Like she was saying good-bye, slow and thorough, but still good-bye. "I'm sorry."

"I know. Me too." I think we were sorry about different things. I stepped a bit further back. My hands were shaking. I tried to button my shirt. The buttons were way too big for the little holes.

"Come here." She used my collar to bring me closer. Then she started buttoning my shirt. With her head bent, her hair tickled my face. "I'm not sure what's wrong with me."

"What do you mean?"

"I can't seem to stay away from you. I think you're trouble." She was studying my now buttoned shirt.

"The good kind or the bad kind?"

"The kind I need to stay away from." Fuck.

"Why don't you then?" I already knew I was making her life complicated. We both knew that. We were also having the same issue. Neither of us could leave the other alone.

"I can't," she said. Her hand settled on my chest right over my heart.

"Wes." She looked at me. "If you want me to go away, I will. But I don't want to." I was surprised to realize I was telling the truth.

"I don't know what to do."

"You could always go out with me." Maybe if I just kept asking she would.

"I can't."

"Seems like there's a lot you can't do."

"I'm sorry." Her hand fell and she stepped back. "I think we just need to keep it simple." She was mumbling, like she didn't believe it.

"If that's what you want." We were way past simple.

"So, friends?" Her gaze dropped back to the floor. It was probably the least sincere offer of friendship I'd ever gotten.

"Sure."

The two of us just stood there staring at each other. Neither believing what the other said. I was also damn sure that she was as turned on as I was. And I was ready to explode. Making out is fun and all, but it's a bit more fun when it leads somewhere.

Her phone rang.

"Damn." She pulled her phone out and answered the call. "What, Trev?" There was a pause and then she looked pissed. "I only asked you to watch him for an hour." I could hear Trevor start talking again. "So you just wanted an excuse to call me. Fine… No, I'll ask her right now." Wes pulled the phone away from her ear. "Trevor wants to know if you want to go pier fishing tomorrow night."

"Just me and Trevor?"

"No, everyone. Theo, Trevor, Jamie." Wes had an issue with frustration. When she was irritated at one person, she was irritated at everyone. You could hear it in her voice. I'm not sure why I found that sexy.

"How 'bout you?"

That got her to smile. "Yeah, me too."

"I'm there." She lifted the phone to her ear to tell Trevor. "Tell him thanks for inviting me."

She nodded. "She's in, Trev. She says thanks for inviting her… He says you're welcome," she said to me. "No, I'm not telling her that." Back to Trevor. "And you have to tell Theo he's gotta take a nap if we're going midnight fishing. He might listen to you. I'll be there soon." She ended the call. "I should probably go."

"Do you know yet why you came?"

"No."

"Did you get what you were looking for?"

"I'm not sure."

CHAPTER NINE

Three guys yelling back and forth to each other in Spanish were set up about three quarters of the way down the pier. They were wearing soccer jerseys and cargo shorts stained with fish guts. It was freezing. They were crazy. I had on torn jeans, a thermal, and my pea coat. Ollie had dressed me because I'd never been fishing before.

Two of the three lights at the end of the pier were out. The remaining one bathed Wes and her little family in an orange glow. Trevor was bouncing between the poles to check them with an exuberant Theo following him. Both radiated the same excitement. Jamie was sprawled in a green canvas chair with a blanket and a book. Wes leaned back against the same bench where we'd nearly kissed only a week before. She was watching the poles too, but with a calmer air.

"Having fun?" I called as I got closer.

"Tons." Wes smiled and my stomach dropped. That was becoming a familiar sensation.

"Catch anything yet?" I leaned against the bench next to her.

"Nothing good. Trev's been here since seven catching bait."

"Seven?" She nodded. "That's like four hours."

"He's obsessed."

"Jamie too?" Jamie looked about ready to die of boredom.

"No, she just got here." Wes lowered her voice to an exaggerated whisper. "I think she hates fishing. Never catches anything."

"Wes, I'm sitting six feet from you," Jamie called without turning around. "At least turn away if you're talking about me."

Wes started grinning and turned her back to Jamie. "So she really sucks, but she comes out here to indulge Trev."

"I hate you." Jamie still didn't turn around.

"You guys should try for sincerity," I said. "It might look good on you."

"Hmm." Wes scrunched up her nose. "No, I don't think it would." Jamie started laughing. Theo and Trevor finally realized I'd joined them.

"Hey, Alden." Trevor looked up from the line he was playing with.

"Hey, Alden," Theo mimicked him. He trotted over to us. "Are you fishing too?"

"I guess. I've never been fishing."

"Never?" Wes and Theo said together. I shook my head. They were dressed almost identically. Again. Both wore a thick dark sweater over a white T-shirt with grubby white Vans and had their hair pulled back. Theo had a little wool jacket over his sweater. He looked like a Gap commercial.

"Do you guys always dress alike?" They looked at each other.

"Wes told me what to wear. She said I need to dress warm," Theo explained.

"I didn't realize we were dressed the same." Wes seemed a little disturbed.

"You guys do it all the time." I thought they were just being cute.

"Nuh-uh." Very convincing, Wes.

"Uh-huh," I responded in kind.

"I did a ponytail 'cause Wes did." Theo pulled at his pretty hair.

Wes stared down at him. "That's why you wanted a ponytail?"

"Yeah. You're my big sis." She kept staring at him. He shrugged and skipped back over to Trevor.

"How cute."

"I always forget how much he looks up to me. It's weird."

"No, it isn't. It's adorable."

"Dude, you guys, I think there's something on my pole," Jamie said. Her book and blanket dropped unceremoniously onto her chair as she rushed to the pole. The end slowly dipped and straightened, then repeated the movement.

"Come on, Jamie. It's your line. It repels fish." Trevor didn't bother to turn around.

"No, Trev. I think she has something." Wes smiled roguishly.

"I do. I really do." Jamie bounced on the balls of her feet.

"Set the hook, Jamie. Reel it in," Wes said.

I followed Wes to the end of the pier. Trevor was still unconvinced. With a sharp jerk, Jamie pulled her pole up and started reeling.

"It's heavy. I bet I got a shark." That made Trevor turn around. He grabbed the light and shone it into the water. Wes lifted Theo and the three of us looked over the edge. The line was centered in a mass of kelp tangled around one of the pillars that disappeared into the waves.

"Looks like it's under the seaweed," Wes said.

"Totally, babe. Reel it in hard. Bring it to the surface." Now Trevor was smiling just like Wes. Whatever they were up to it wasn't good.

"All right. It's heavy, you guys." Jamie wrestled with the line. "Is someone gonna get the net?" Trevor and Wes didn't move. She wrestled with her line and waited for help that wasn't coming.

"Jamie, you got kelp," Theo finally said.

"No way," she protested. The seaweed started to rise above the water attached to the line. "Man."

The light switched off and I looked up in time to see Wes set Theo back down then erupt into laughter with Trevor. They high-fived each other before both doubled over.

"You guys knew," Jamie screamed. "That's mean."

"That's pretty messed up, you guys." They were unmoved by my criticism. The effort to stand became too much so they leaned against each other still howling.

Theo joined Jamie and patted her arm. "It's okay, Jamie. Next time you'll get a shark." He was too damn sweet.

"Thanks, honey." Jamie abandoned the pole, its line still hanging over the edge. "Come here, T." She glared at Trevor. "Trev will clean my line." She sat back in her chair and Theo climbed into her lap.

"You did real good setting the hook and stuff." Theo continued to comfort her.

"I thought so too." The pair settled in to watch.

Wes and Trevor got their giggling under control enough to reel the line in. They set about the task of removing the kelp and throwing it into the lone trashcan.

"Alden, you want to rig this with me? It'll be your pole." Wes was holding the line in one hand and a knife in the other. A couple butchered sardines rested on the railing in front of her.

"No, thanks."

"What?" Apparently, she wasn't expecting an argument.

"I don't think I want you or Trevor teaching me to fish." Trevor turned when he heard his name and he and Wes just stared at me. Jamie started laughing.

"Why?"

"Are you kidding? I saw what you guys did to Jamie." Even though I tried to keep it in check, I was grinning.

"Oh, whatever," she scoffed when she realized I wasn't serious. "Get over here."

"Fine. What do I do?" She let me help attach a couple hooks and weights to the line.

"You want me to put on the bait for you?" Wes pointed at the sardines with fluid leaking from their bellies. It was a test.

"I got it, thanks." I chose a chunk and slid it on the bottom hook. Hey, I was a chef. Raw fish wasn't going to get me going. I was pretty sure she was impressed. When each hook was baited, Wes walked me to the side of the pier.

"You know how to cast?" I shook my head. "All right, hold the pole in your hand and with the other, grip right here." She placed my right hand above the reel. "Hook your finger around the line and flip this up." Her right hand now rested lightly on top of mine so she could demonstrate the appropriate way to hold the line. With her other hand she flipped up a piece of metal holding the line in place.

"Got it."

"So you check behind you before you cast." We both looked behind us at the deserted pier. Theo was still sitting with Jamie, and Trevor was pacing back and forth between the poles. "Now you're going to cast it sideways. Brace the pole against your forearm, and when you toss it out, let go of the line with your finger. Once the line sinks, you put this back down." She indicated the piece of metal she'd just flipped up.

"All right." I held the pole at the indicated angle and let the line fly like I was told.

"Awesome." There was a splash and my line slowed a bit. She was still standing close with her hand on my forearm. The line was still going so I stopped it like I'd been told. "Now you set your pole down and wait. Keep an eye on it. If the tip goes down really sharply then you probably have something. But don't get too excited 'cause the waves will also make it move a bit."

"So what do we do now?"

"Wait."

❖

"Wes, I'm cold." Theo burrowed into her.

"Are you sleepy?" She brushed a rebellious curl off his forehead.

"No. Just cold." He pushed his face further into her stomach.

"You want to know a trick to keep warm?" I knelt next to him.

"Okay." He abandoned Wes to stand in front of me.

"If you flip your collar up, it will keep your neck warm." I popped his collar so it sheltered his neck. "And if you take down your ponytail, your hair will keep your ears warm." He tugged out his hair tie and handed it to Wes. I finger combed his hair forward so it covered his ears. "Better?"

"Yeah," he said with a shy smile. "Thanks."

Wes and I watched him run back to Jamie.

"You're good with him."

"I'm winging it."

"Then your instincts are good."

"Thanks." Fleetingly, she ran her hand down my arm. "He's right. It's freezing." It was nearing midnight and a fog was rolling in.

"Yeah, it's pretty cold." Wes was still just wearing a sweater.

"You want my jacket?"

She looked at me like I was crazy. "Then you'll freeze." At my shrug, she smiled. "Chivalrous is cute on you."

"Great, I always wanted to be cute," I said with a grimace.

"Besides, if I catch something I won't be able to do anything if I'm wearing a jacket."

"How about my thermal? I've got a shirt under it."

"No, I'm all right." She wrapped her arms around herself. "I'm just glad I made Theo wear a coat."

"Come on, Wes." I could tell she wasn't going to give in. "Here. Hold this." I shrugged the jacket down my arms and handed it to her. Then I stripped off the long sleeve under it.

"Seriously. I'm fine."

"No, you're not." I took my jacket back and handed her the shirt.

"Thanks." Reluctantly, she took the thermal. I held her sweater while she put on my shirt. It was a bit long for her, but it was still tight enough to layer her sweater over it.

"Better?"

"Much."

"Hey, Wes. You might have something," Trevor called as Wes pulled the garment over her head.

"No way." We went to her pole. After watching the tip dip abruptly a few times Wes jerked the pole back and started reeling. "Oh, yeah. I way got something."

"What is it?" Trevor peered into the water.

"Dude, it's so a shark," she responded.

"Move over, Trev. I got the light." Jamie muscled Trevor out of the way to illuminate the dark water.

The last six feet of the pier didn't have railings. Instead, wood boards created a waist-high wall. Theo was trying to jump up, but there was no way for him to see.

"Hey, Theo." He turned toward me. "You want me to lift you?"

"Yeah."

We moved down far enough so that everyone else would have room to maneuver. Trevor was behind us untangling the line on the crab net. Below us, we could barely see the line as it moved in a circle through the water.

"Whoa. Look," Theo shouted and pointed. Dark fins were visible for a second before they dipped back below the surface. "Did you see that?" He glanced back at me.

"Yeah. That's way cool, huh?"

He nodded then returned his attention to the water.

Next to us, Trevor started lowering the net. "Keep it steady, Wes."

"I'm trying, but I can't see it." She gave Jamie the death look.

"I can't keep the light on it if it keeps moving," Jamie tossed back.

"Just shut up and keep it steady. Both of you." Trevor dropped the net below the surface. Just as quickly, he started pulling it up. "Dude, I missed it."

"There it is." Theo pointed. The shark turned on its side displaying the line between dark gray and smooth white. "Cool."

Trevor dipped the net again and pulled up. "Got it. Got it. Help me with this."

Wes set down her pole and started pulling the rope up with Trevor. "Theo, when we pull this up you need to stay back."

"Why?"

"'Cause I don't want it to bite you."

When the net came over the side, I backed up with Theo still in my arms. Wes grabbed the tail and dropped it in a clear area.

"It's a female." She sounded pissed. "It swallowed the hook."

"Guess it was hungry," Trevor responded ingeniously.

"You know what that means." Jamie joined them in a semicircle around the shark. "Guess we're having shark tomorrow."

I set Theo down and we joined them, standing a couple feet away. Theo leaned back against me and I set my hands on his shoulders.

"All right, get me the knife." Wes pushed up her sleeves and held out her hand.

Jamie handed her the knife and Trevor lightly stepped on its head.

Wes sliced through the line that disappeared in its mouth. Then she kneeled down and quickly cut the head off. It sounded like she was sawing through sandpaper rather than skin and cartilage. "Back up, Trev." He jumped out of the way. She grabbed the tail and held the body over the water, shaking it so it would bleed out. "Theo, stay with Alden. The head can still bite."

"Okay, Wes." The severed end of the head was facing toward Theo and me. The bloody muscles were flexing, like it was gasping for air. "Does it hurt the shark?" Theo asked me, his eyes still riveted to the head.

"Not anymore. Your sister did it quick so it wouldn't hurt."

"Why is it moving?" The jaws started opening and closing.

"There's something called nerves in the head that make it do that."

Wes gave the body one last shake and set it back on the pier. Efficiently, she cut the belly open. Blood and white fluid seeped from the wound. The knife dropped to the pier and Wes pawed through the organs until she found what she was looking for. A long, creamy white sac a little bigger than her hand. She ran her fingers over it.

"Wes? Should we throw it back?" For the first time, Trevor didn't sound excited. They were afraid it was pregnant.

"No, we're good," she said with relief. With the panache of a surgeon, Wes picked up her knife and stripped the shark of its innards. As a chef, I could appreciate how efficiently she gutted it. Actually, I found it kind of sexy. I was a little warped.

"See if you can find the rig," Trevor joked, his humor restored now that he knew they hadn't killed the next generation.

"You mean this rig?" Wes triumphantly handed him some slimy hooks tied together.

"Gross." He held the hook up to the light and inspected the entrails hanging from it.

Once finished with disemboweling the fish, Wes began cleaning up. Each organ made a nice splash as Wes tossed it over the railing. She wiped the knife on the railing. For a second, she looked like she was going to just throw it on top of their gear, but with a glance at Theo, she slid it into a sheath and properly stowed it. Her hands and arms were covered to the elbow with shark gunk. With a jerk of her arms, she tried unsuccessfully to fling it off.

"Heads up, Wes." Trevor threw a towel to her.

"Thanks." A look of disgust fixed itself to her beautiful face. "I don't mind gutting it, but this is just wrong."

"Wes?" Theo was still leaning against me.

"Yeah?" The dirty towel landed on top of the gear.

"I gotta pee."

"Good timing, T. I want to wash my hands." She smelled them. "That's rank. Anyone want to walk with us? That bathroom scares me."

"I'll go with you guys." I finally let Theo go. The shark head was still on the pier, but he went straight to Wes.

"Cool." The three of us headed down the pier with Theo running ahead then back to us. In his high-pitched voice he recounted blow-by-blow the tale of his amazing sister the shark catcher. At the end of the pier was a cement structure that looked like it could survive a nuclear attack.

They sauntered in and I followed closely behind. The bathroom was freaky. A couple of flickering lights illuminated the stalls, a single cracked mirror, and sinks that had seen better centuries. The entire place looked ideal for filming a horror flick. Wes kicked all the stall doors open to make sure it was empty then let Theo run in to do his business.

After washing her hands, she called to Theo, "T, we're going to be outside waiting."

"Okay." His voice echoed off the walls.

We'd only been out half a minute before Theo ran out of the bathroom.

"You wash your hands?" Wes asked.

"Yep. By myself."

I couldn't imagine who would have helped him.

"Good job."

With that, we started back down the pier. Where the sand became the waves beneath us, we stopped by some unspoken agreement. Theo climbed onto the railing to stare at the water, and Wes stood directly behind him, holding him in place. Moonlight caught on the cresting waves below us stretching along the shore until it disappeared. Everything else remained dark except for that streak of silver. It seemed to absorb the light rather than reflect it.

"That's pretty." Only a five-year-old could use so few words to describe the ocean in moonlight.

In response, Wes ruffled his hair. Our shoulders just barely touched so that the three of us were linked.

"All right. You guys ready to head back?"

I wasn't sure I wanted to, but I agreed anyway. Theo nodded and took off down the pier again.

"We can leave T with Trev and Jamie and walk on the beach if you want." Wes stared straight ahead, keeping an eye on Theo.

"Sure. That'd be cool," I said even though I didn't know why she would want to walk with me. Moonlit beaches were reserved for old couples and young lovers. Neither applied.

CHAPTER TEN

When we reached the end of the pier, Trevor was waiting with a pole for Theo to help cast. Satisfied that he was occupied, Wes grabbed my hand and pulled me back down the pier. She called to them as we walked away, "Guys, we'll be back. We're going for a walk."

They nodded in our direction before Trevor resumed wildly gesturing the proper technique for casting on the pier. Theo mimed the action, earning him a hearty pat on the back. I glanced at Wes watching him. The look on her face was enough to break my heart. She seriously loved the kid.

A second later, she turned and continued yanking me down the pier. When we stepped onto the sand, my feet sank and the chill seeped into my shoes.

"Damn, it's cold out here." I flipped up the collar on my pea coat and stuffed my hands in my pockets. Wes linked her arm through mine and directed me into the dark under the pier.

"You should feel it in January." She glanced down pensively at her foot. "I can't feel my big toe."

Experimentally, I wiggled my toes. "Me either." Halfway down to the water I stopped, leaned against one of the wooden pillars, and held open my coat. "Put your hands in my jacket. It's warm." Swear, I was just being nice.

Wes looked at me like I was crazy.

"I'm serious. Come on."

"All right." I could tell she was skeptical, but she leaned closer to me and threaded her arms around my waist. The curve of her lips lifted into a small smile that was just barely visible in the sparse light. There was a tug at the back of my shirt and I tensed up trying to pull away. She pressed her palms against the bare skin of my lower back.

"Oh, shit, that's freezing." My voice was a bit higher than usual.

"Mmm, you're right. You are warm."

"It's my main attribute." I struggled to keep my breathing even. I was torn between leaning into the sensation of her hands on me and recoiling from the cold. When her palms had leeched all the warmth from my back she drew her hands along my sides to rest them on my stomach. The feather-light touch just below my ribs made me jump.

"No way." Her grin widened until I could see her one dimple. "Are you ticklish?"

"No," I said quickly. She immediately squeezed the soft spot between my hips and ribs. I jumped about and yelped. "No fair." I tried to grab her hands and remove them from my shirt, but she did it again. "Stop, stop. Please." There was no mercy.

She started laughing so I did too. My back was pressed into the pillar again so I couldn't get away from her. Not that I didn't try. With every movement, she pinned me harder. I finally got purchase on one hand, but she twisted out of my grasp until she had both my wrists trapped. She pulled down on them so I would stop struggling. The movement brought me within an inch of her face. Bad idea. I could smell oranges in her hair like before, but also a sweet spice like Christmas. It seemed her eyes were the only source of illumination under the pier. All I could see was blue-green light drawing me in. I leaned closer until my lips were poised over hers. Warm breath cascaded over my mouth. The heat radiating from her scorched me and I knew I would never feel cold again.

"Alden, don't," she said. The words brushed across my lips like a wistful caress.

"Why?" I didn't pull away. I couldn't. Her eyes paralyzed me.

"You know why."

I did. I knew exactly why. I did it anyway. If her breath scorched, the kiss incinerated. All I could think about was that she was kissing me back. Then I just stopped thinking. She dropped my hands and I slid them into her hair. Her lips tasted the same as before—kind of salty and sweet. The ocean couldn't be washed off her. It was in her blood. Where my thumb rested against her neck I could feel the push-pull of the waves pumping through her veins. Her hands migrated to my back again just low enough to tuck her fingers under the waistband of my boxers.

"Fuck." I was pretty sure I only stayed standing because she was holding me there. "I have a proposition."

"You want to proposition me? I'm sure this will be good." There was some serious sarcasm in her voice. Under that, I could tell she wanted me bad.

Here goes. "Come home with me." She was smiling. "No, seriously. You want to. You know I want to. We can have rules if you want. Break my heart if you feel the need. Just please…I have to touch you or I think I'll go crazy." She needed convincing, I could tell.

"What kind of rules?" Her fingers were still stuck in my boxers. While we talked, she dragged them back and forth at an agonizingly slow pace.

"Whatever kind you want." It would probably kill me, but why not? I'd do anything she wanted.

"Are you serious?" Her hands stilled.

"Or no rules. We could just get carried away." I grinned. "That could be fun too." I kissed her again. Kissed her until I knew there wasn't much sense left in her head. Kissed her until those hands started moving again. I'd take that as a yes. I did a mental woo-hoo. Not that I was sure what the hell was going on.

"One night." Ouch. "One night to try to get you out of my head."

"I don't think one night will get you out of mine." But worth a shot.

"I'm not sure I can give you more than that," she said and shrugged. It hurt. She knew it was killing me. I nodded. That pain should have slowed me down. It didn't. When her lips took mine again, I forgot. I forgot about everything. Her hands slid up and cupped my breasts, twisting and pulling at my nipples. I leaned my head back and bit my lip to hold back a groan. Weston took the opportunity to lick my neck from the collar of my shirt up to the edge of my jaw.

"That's it." I grabbed her arms and removed the questing hands from my shirt. Then I pinned them to her sides and kissed her. I walked forward forcing her back until she was up against a pillar. I restrained myself as long as possible before I touched my tongue to hers. Her mouth was warm and soft. Our bodies were still separated by a few inches of air. The only points of contact were our lips and hands. Wes grabbed my jacket and yanked me closer. Our bodies cleaved together. I pressed my thigh between her legs, making her moan.

"Alden, stop. Fuck," she breathed before pushing my shoulders back so I couldn't kiss her anymore. From the waist down we were still melded together.

"You started it," I complained indignantly.

She held my shoulders back so I couldn't get any closer. "We can't make out under the pier," she said.

I smiled in what was hopefully a charming way. "Uh-huh. See, we got the pier and that's half the challenge. Now we just need to make out." I leaned down and captured her mouth again. My tongue traced along her bottom lip before I sucked it into my mouth. There is something about making out under a pier that is just so fifteen-years-old-and-horny that you can't resist doing it.

I relinquished the soft skin to whisper, "Want to get out of here? I promise what I have planned is way more fun than fishing on the pier."

She bit her lip and nodded. "Let me give Trevor my car keys. I'll be right back."

❖

I thought I was going to die on the drive to Weston's. Restraint's not my strong suit. Not hers either. Two blocks from the house, her seatbelt was off and she was nearly in my lap. I struggled to watch the road as Wes licked the top of my ear then bit the lobe.

When she pushed her tongue inside my ear, I gasped. My spine tingled. "Fuck. I'm trying to drive here."

She laughed, a smooth, deep noise in her throat. The sound made my clit twitch, bringing to my attention the pressure from the seam of my boxers. The advantage of sagging your pants is that usually they're low enough to eliminate that problem. If you sit at the wrong angle, you're screwed. I was screwed.

"Stop, stop. Need to drive." I pushed her back with one hand. "Please." I tried to focus my blurry vision on the road. "Fuck, I think I'm about to come."

Reluctantly, Wes slid back to her seat. I risked a glance in her direction. Her hand twitched on her thigh, and the slightly belligerent look on her face inspired me to study the road with fervor.

I pushed back in my seat a fraction of an inch so my underwear would stop rubbing. My knuckles were white on the steering wheel with the effort of continuing to drive as my body melted. Wes wasn't even touching me anymore, but my nerve endings were on fire. We got to her house and I pulled my truck into the driveway. In one movement, the brake was on, my seatbelt was off, and I was out of the car. She watched me curiously.

"Get out of the truck," I said loud enough for her to hear me through the window. She looked at me like I was crazy. "We're not fucking on my front seat, and if I'm within touching distance I can't promise much, so get out of the truck."

Wes got out and slammed the door as I came around to her side. "You can't touch me either." She held out her arm to push me away. "Besides, I need a shower."

"What? Why?" That was like five more minutes of waiting.

"We were just fishing."

"So?"

"So I gutted a shark."

"Fine." That made sense. I tried for a stubborn pout. She laughed.

At the door, Wes turned to put the key in the lock. I brushed her hair aside enough to suck on the patch of skin at the nape of her neck.

She shuddered and pulled away. "If you want to do this inside, you better stop."

I just laughed.

Wes pushed the door open. There were no lights on in the house. She pushed the coat off my shoulders and tossed it in the direction of the closet. I followed her up the stairs so close behind her we almost fell back down. In the hallway, I cupped her breasts forcing her to push back into me. She groaned and pulled away holding me at arm's length until we were in her room with the door closed.

"Stay," she commanded in a tone slightly better than one uses with a dog. I think I whined in response.

My back was glued to the door. Her sweater dropped to the ground. My thermal followed. I decided it would be prudent to stay put. The T-shirt was next. My hands were sweating. They slid down the door. She lost her bra. There was something so damn sexy about a chick wearing nothing but boxers and jeans. The jeans were tight and slung low enough to show a couple inches of her boxer briefs. I wear boxers, the others are too tight, but I like the view and Wes made them look damn good. Her hips rose above the tight material creating shadows across her smooth skin. One of her shoes hit me in the leg.

"Stop staring." The other shoe hit me in the stomach.

"Uh-uh. I can't."

She leaned against the doorframe of the bathroom to peel off her jeans. Still wearing her boxer briefs, she disappeared through the doorway. I waited, attempting to count to ten. The underwear were tossed out the door. Six, I made it to six. The shower turned on. In the few seconds it took to cross the room Wes was already in the shower.

"You can't come in."

"Why not?" I was taking off my shoes.

"'Cause I said."

"I'm watching then."

"No, you aren't."

"Yes, I am. You watched me shower."

"That was different."

"Too bad." I adopted a good stance to watch. Feet planted, my thumb tucked into the waistband of my jeans, my other hand rested on my stomach under my shirt. As she washed, my hand drifted aimlessly up and down. The muscles in my stomach started to flutter so I stopped. I remembered the shower Wes had witnessed. The way I'd gotten so turned on having her watch me. I think she was feeling the same way. I sure as hell was. The water shut off. When she stepped out toweling her hair dry, I panicked. For weeks, I couldn't sleep properly, I'd been constantly wet, I'd done everything possible to get her just talking to me, and then there she was standing in front of me with nothing except a towel. Since she was drying her hair with it, there wasn't much coverage. Fuck, she was sexy. The lines of her ribs that tilted up into perfect breasts with dark pink, almost brown nipples. Her skin was an unblemished gold highlighted by a light dust of freckles down her nose and across her shoulders. She looked too good, too perfect, too damn sexy. That's what made me panic.

When she crossed the room and stopped in front of me, all other thoughts fled. That towel hung between us, a tenuous connection. It landed on my now bare feet. Her body pressed against mine. Warm, wet skin against cool denim.

"You're getting my clothes wet."

"Damn right." Her tongue traced along my bottom lip. "Now lose them."

I took a step back. Those damn eyes studied every inch of skin I exposed until there was nothing left, just me. Solid wood of the bed frame hit my calves. I didn't remember walking backward. She pushed me down, then hovered a breath above me. A knee planted on either side framed her sex above my stomach. I waited to see if she would move. Her control was impeccable. I traced my fingertips up the outside of her thighs, past her hips, around her belly button, writing a story on her skin. Goose bumps trailed in the wake of my touch. When I allowed my palms to graze the hard tips of her nipples, her breathing became erratic. Still she maintained her stance, suspended above me. She seemed fascinated by the muscles twitching in my stomach the more I touched her. I had no secrets.

My damn body described in every movement how much I was holding in.

"Do you know how much I want you?" she said.

All I could do was shake my head. Long fingers wrapped around my wrist and dragged me back down her flesh to the apex of her thighs. Moisture saturated my hand with a simple touch. Her eyes flickered shut when I traced a finger around her clit.

"You're going to," she breathed as I pressed hard enough to make her twitch. "Oh, fuck." I circled again. "Make me come."

"Oh, no. Not that, not yet." I stopped touching her long enough to cup both my hands behind her neck, pull her head down, and kiss her thoroughly before releasing her. In one smooth motion, I slid beneath her hooking my arms around her thighs. I bit the patch of shaved skin. She began to writhe above me. The smell of her desire seeped into me. I waited.

"Please, Alden," Wes murmured as she lost patience.

So I took her into my mouth. I sucked on her flesh until she screamed. Her fingers were twitching in my hair. I licked the length of her clit, allowing my tongue ring to catch and drag, teasing until a sob escaped her. The muscles in her legs tightened against my grip. I continued my devotions until I couldn't feel a damn thing except the pressure of her thighs against my head and the soft skin filling my mouth and the liquid dripping down my throat. The second before she exploded, I let go and pushed my fingers deep inside her, milking her orgasm with my tongue and hands until her cries softened to murmurs and she collapsed onto the bed.

I thought I was fine. I really did. The way she'd fallen, her lips were inches away, her leg was pressed between mine, and one perfect hand rested between my breasts. I was watching that hand when I felt her shift. A warm tongue traced along the edge of my ear. A shiver spread through my body. That was my spot. How did she know that? My heart rate went through the roof. She had to feel it with her palm pressed to my chest.

"You like that?" Her tone was gentle, mocking, and so damn sexy.

"A bit," I managed to respond.

"You're shaved too." The hand on my chest slid down and started tracing the edge of where I should have had hair.

"You noticed."

Her hand continued to wander, smoothing down my thigh and back up again, scratching slowly, carefully along my skin. I shivered every time she stopped so close to where I wanted her. When she finally, finally slid warm fingers through the wetness, I arched off the bed. She kissed me as she teased me. Her tongue tracing over my lips desperately, fleetingly, pushing into my mouth and pulling away. The tips of her fingers played at my entrance and I whimpered. I was close, so close that I knew the second she slid inside I would come, and I did. Filled, pushed to the point of breaking, control out the fucking window came with her pressed against my sweat-slicked skin, pressed deep inside me so all I knew was her.

CHAPTER ELEVEN

Sweat soaked through my boxers, drenching the waistband of my jeans. The white T-shirt I was wearing also clung to my damp skin. With every drop into the half pipe, the sea air buffeted my body making my shirt flap against my back until I came to rest on the other side of the ramp. My session had started with simple stalls, resting the nose of my board against the pipe built into the top of the ramp, holding and dropping in again.

Now, hours later, I was desperately practicing tricks I'd done for years just to sink into the monotony, the repetition I knew. Grinds where my board would straddle the edge as it slid away beneath me, or where I'd balance at just the right angle to glide on one truck before spinning back onto the ramp and continue to the other side. Anything, anything to sweat it out, sweat her out.

I didn't feel it, though. Not the ramp or the pipe or the grip tape when I touched my board. She ruined me so the only things I felt were soft skin and a different sort of wetness, the silky, heady kind. That didn't make me stop trying. Used to be, when I skated I was consumed by the speed and rush when I became airborne, lost as my trucks slid over a waxed bar. Instead, I felt nothing.

After a particularly flamboyant spin that I couldn't land, I skidded down the ramp on my knees. My jeans, which had been wearing thin, finally tore. My knee, exposed now, scraped the ramp leaving behind a layer of skin. Shit, that stung. I'd already pulled a similar number on my elbow and I'd smacked the back of my head pretty good. Fuck that. I collected my board, couldn't find my pride so I left without it.

"Ollie, you here?" I yelled as I pushed through the backdoor of Delma's.

"In my office."

I followed the sound of her voice until I found her working at her laptop. "Hey." Exhausted, I slumped into a chair.

"Shit. What happened to you?" She came around the side of the desk to gawk at me.

"I was skating."

"You're bleeding everywhere."

"I fell." She was right, but my jeans were soaking it up and my elbow was already scabbing over. Perspiration dripped from my hair into my eyes. I pushed my hair back, then used my sleeve to wipe my face.

"You look like hell." Her nose wrinkled. Ollie hated when I got all sweaty.

"Come on. I'll drive you home." It wasn't an option.

"It's cool. I got my board."

"Get your ass moving, McKenna." Ollie was so touchy.

"Fine."

"Wait." She disappeared.

"Now what?"

"Put that on your knee." A towel was tossed through the doorway and landed on my lap.

I complied, cinching the towel right below my knee where it bled the most. Then I followed her to the car. All I wanted was a shower and sleep. In the front seat, I leaned back and closed my eyes.

"We're here." Ollie shook my shoulder a little to wake me.

"Cool. Thanks for the ride." When I got out Ollie did too. "What are you doing?"

"I know you're not going to clean up your knee or elbow, so I am."

"Shit, dude. I'm capable of taking care of myself."

All she did was roll her eyes and keep walking. Whatever. I left Ollie on my couch and took a shower. A long shower. My body ached, not from skating for hours or staying up most of the night, rather the ache in my head, the one from wanting Wes, was spreading through me. The shower didn't make it stop.

Covered only by the towel around my waist, I emerged from the bathroom. Ollie waited until I had boxers and a shirt on then forced me back into the bathroom. She rooted around under the sink until she found a bottle of peroxide and some Band-Aids.

"Let me see that." There was an undercurrent of frustration in her voice that I didn't get.

I sat on the counter and let her inspect my leg. The gash extended from the bottom half of my knee about four inches down my shin. Most of the bleeding had stopped in the shower, leaving the skin pink and raw, but blood still seeped from a couple places.

"Hold your knee over the sink."

"I don't want to." I didn't like peroxide.

"Don't be a girl. It won't sting."

In response, I pursed my lips and shook my head. That made her grin. With surprising strength, she cupped a hand around my calf and spun me around on the counter. I closed my eyes and waited. She poured peroxide straight from the bottle until half my leg was dripping. Then she dabbed around the scrape to get rid of the excess.

"Don't touch that. It needs to dry. Let me see your elbow now."

"Ollie, it's fine. It isn't even bleeding anymore."

"You still need to clean it."

"I took a shower."

She rolled her eyes again. "I'm sure that killed whatever lives on those skate ramps."

"Whatever, dude." I turned my arm so she could look at my elbow. "See, it's fine."

"Sure it is." With that, she saturated my elbow with peroxide too. It didn't sting. My aversion was probably psychological. "Glow in the dark?" She inspected one of my boxes of Band-Aids.

"Don't mock my Band-Aids."

"Is your knee dry yet?"

"I think so." Carefully, I probed it. "Yeah."

Ollie placed a large square Band-Aid right below my knee where the gash was the worst. Under that she placed two more across my shin where it was still bleeding. After inspecting my elbow again, she decided it didn't need any further attention.

"There. You're all set."

"Thanks, Ollie." I stood. "I'm gonna find pants." She nodded and started putting stuff away. I pulled on a fresh pair of jeans, collapsed on the couch, and waited for Ollie. I might have fallen asleep again.

"Now, McKenna, you can tell me what the hell is wrong with you." I opened my eyes to find her standing in front of me with her hands on her hips looking royally pissed.

"Huh?"

"You only skate until you're bloody and falling down when something is going on in that head of yours. I want to know." We'd had this conversation before. Ollie thought it was self-destructive. I thought it was healthier than a lot of other things.

"Nothing."

"Tell me." Serious voice. Now I was in for it.

"I umm…" I kiss and tell. So did Ollie. We never left out any sordid details. That might have been wrong, but it was what we did. For once, I had no desire to spill. Like if I shared it wouldn't be real, or worse, it would. Still, I had to tell her something. "It's just Wes."

"Did something happen when you were fishing?"

"No," I said too fast. "Well, yes. We slept together."

"What?" she screamed.

"Ollie, don't, all right? I just…I just don't want to talk about it." Something in my tone must have gotten to her because she opened then closed her mouth and nodded. I just couldn't tell Ollie. I couldn't tell her that when I left I knew that Wes regretted it, regretted me, and that hurt like fucking hell.

"Are you okay?"

"I'm cool." She raised an eyebrow. "All right. I'm terrible. I just don't want to talk."

"Fine." Uh-oh, that meant she was pissed.

"Come on. It's not you. I just need to sulk."

"Alone or with me?" With a question like that there was only one answer. Like if a chick asks if she looks fat, automatic response, no.

"Alone." Wrong answer.

"I love you." She ruffled my wet hair. "Call me."

"I will."

❖

A week later, Wes called.

"Hey, Alden." Her voice cut through me, immediately turning every cell into fire. My hands started sweating and I nearly dropped the phone.

"Hey."

"I, uh, haven't seen you at Lucy's."

"I've been working a lot." It was true, but we both knew that wasn't the reason. I'd been avoiding the place. When a girl informs you that you're having a one-night stand, it's a little rude to keep following her around. Best to disappear for a while. Especially if you don't have anything to offer her.

"Oh." She paused. "Theo is having a sleepover at his friend's tomorrow." So? "And the waves down the coast are supposed to be killer. Doyouwannacome?" she asked in a rush.

"Don't you want to take Trevor or Jamie?"

"No. I want you." Fuck, did she have to say it like that?

"Okay." Like I had a choice.

A whoosh of air came over the line, like she let out a big breath. "For real?"

"Yeah, what time?" I was a masochist.

"Come over at one. We can drop Theo off then drive down."

"I'll be there."

❖

As I waited on her doorstep I remembered the last time I'd rung her doorbell. It was hard not to because my life, it seemed like, had changed then. I was praying in a way that it was about to change again. My week of solitude had shown me one thing. What it felt like to truly hunger for someone. What my life could be without her, a dull ache in my belly that could only be filled with one kind of sustenance.

"Who's there?" a small voice called through the door.

"It's Alden." The lock clicked and the door swung wide.

"Hi." Theo stood there grinning. "I asked like Wes told me."

"Good job." I ruffled his hair to reassure him of his good deed.

"Wes is out back. She's waxing her board." He took my hand and towed me into the kitchen.

Through the open back door I could see Wes. She looked fuckin' hot. The sleeves of her shirt were pushed up so I could see the play of muscles in her arms as she massaged the wax into her board. Damn.

"Did you eat?" Theo climbed up to the table. He kneeled on one of the chairs and surveyed the spread in front of him. Peanut butter, bread, jam, the essentials.

"Uh, no. I guess not." Was Red Bull food?

"You gotta. It's fuel." He looked at me like I should have known. "Wes said so."

"Then it must be true," I said seriously.

"Uh huh. She knows everything." We both nodded. "Do you want PB and J? I can make it."

"That sounds great." I wasn't hungry and I hadn't eaten a peanut butter sandwich since I was about seven. "We should make one for Wes too."

"Okay." A big smile took over his face. That killed me, the way he smiled. It was like watching a little Wes.

"Can you open this?" He handed the bread to me.

"Sure." I pulled the plastic tab off and handed the bag back to him. Wheat bread. Not many kids like that. With his small hands, he pulled out six slices of bread, one at a time, and set them on the cutting board in front of him. I opened the peanut butter and set the open container next to the cutting board.

"Thanks." With precision, he took up a butter knife and started swiping peanut butter over the bread in front of him. He was concentrating hard, if his tongue sticking out the corner of his mouth was any indication. "Can you open this?" He handed me the jam.

"Sure." My role was clearly that of assistant, one I was happy to fill. "Do you need me to do anything else?"

"Prolly." He nodded. Slowly, he placed the sticky sides of the bread together. "'Cause I can't cut them." A dramatic frown crossed his face complete with a furrowed brow and pouty lips. Life was tough as a five-year-old.

"Not a problem." I grabbed a big kid knife from the counter. "How do you want them cut?"

"Like this." He crossed his hands in an X.

"Like this?" I indicated the cuts with the knife.

"Yeah."

With the necessary approval, I cut each sandwich as he carefully placed them in front of me. His knuckles were painted dark red from the mouth of the jam jar.

"Hey, Theo, your hands are sticky." He glanced at his palms. "On the other side, dude." He flipped them and grinned.

"I got jam on 'em." Clearly, he wasn't concerned.

I picked up the knife that was still covered in peanut butter and swiped a finger through it. "Oh no, it looks like you got some on your nose too." I painted a streak of peanut butter down his nose.

He giggled and looked mildly appalled. "You got it on my nose."

"No, I didn't."

"Uh-huh. Like this." He grabbed the spoon, wiped off some jam, and carefully drew it down my nose. Then he erupted into giggles. A small food fight ensued. Theo ended up on my lap with me tickling his armpits as he screamed between bouts of laughter for mercy. I could feel a sticky hand print on my face and I was pretty sure we both had peanut butter in our hair. Wes came to the door, probably because we were being loud.

"Hey, you two. What gives?" Wes yelled to be heard over us. She was grinning almost as much as Theo and I were.

"Umm." Theo gasped for breath. "We made peanut butter and jelly." He offered as an explanation.

"I can see that. But why did you make it on your faces?"

Theo started giggling again. "Alden started it."

"You sold me out." I tickled him some more.

"Maybe we should eat the PB and J instead of wearing it." Wes smiled even bigger. "We have to go soon." So responsible.

"Okay," Theo said. "We made you one too."

"Thanks, T." Wes pulled out a chair across from us. I lifted Theo off my lap and onto his chair.

Anyone who wants to reclaim their youth should eat peanut butter and jelly. I felt ten years younger eating mine, but maybe not in a good way. Theo carefully dissected his sandwich instead of just eating it. First, he ate the crust off every piece, then he bit off the corners of each triangle until he had four circles. The circles were popped into his mouth with a flourish, like candy. Kids are weird.

"If you guys want to go wash your faces and stuff I'll clean up in here," Wes said as Theo polished off his sandwich.

"All right. Come on, T." I circled an arm around his waist and threw him over my shoulder. With my free hand I started tickling him again, but that made his feet flail around very close to my face so I stopped. That's when I saw his ankles. They were bruised and scraped up. The bruises had been accumulated over time because some were yellow and some were a fresh purple. I set him on his feet and was about to ask what they were from when I realized.

"Do you skateboard?"

"Uh-course." Duh, everyone skateboarded.

"You gotta wear high-tops, dude."

"I keep telling him that. It looks like I beat him." Wes grabbed Theo under his arms and swung him in the air, then turned him upside down.

"Weessss, nooo." He giggled and screamed. She inspected the bruised area then kissed his ankles. "It's better now. It's better." He continued to protest. Laughing, she set him down.

"Why don't you wear high-tops?" I asked him. "Vans makes some cool ones."

"'Cause I can't tie 'em." Duh.

"Got it." I looked around a bit. I didn't know where anything was. "So uhh…"

"Bathroom's upstairs." Wes nodded toward the stairs then grinned. "Have fun."

I wasn't entirely sure what that meant so I let Theo lead the way.

"This is my bathroom." He flipped the light switch that was eye level for him. The whole room was *Finding Nemo*, from the shower curtain to his toothbrush. "I like Nemo," he explained.

"Cool. Me too." I helped Theo wash his face with a washcloth, which I also used to remove the peanut butter from his hair.

"Uh oh." Theo was looking down.

"What?"

"I got it on my shirt." Sure enough, there was a streak across his shirt.

"Better take it off and find a new one." I turned back to the sticky mess that was now my hair.

"Okay." He stripped off the shirt and placed it in a laundry hamper behind the door. Instead of going to get a new shirt, he just watched me.

"Are you gonna get a shirt?"

"I don't like shirts."

"You had one on before."

"It got dirty." Maybe this was what Wes meant. I wondered if she was just being funny or if this was a test. Like to see if I could get the kid to wash and change or not. I doubted it, but still.

"Aren't you going to a sleepover?"

"Yeah."

"Have any of your friends come to a sleepover without a shirt?" It was the best I could come up with.

"No." He tilted his head to one side, studying me. "Guess I'll go get one." He ran off and returned moments later wearing a shirt.

We went back downstairs to find Wes waiting for us.

"Are we goin'?" Theo asked as he jumped the last two steps.

"Don't jump on the stairs, T. And calm down. We still have to tie the boards on the car."

"That'll take for-eh-verrr." With each syllable his shoulders and head dropped a couple inches.

"We can just take mine if you want." I tried to tell Wes quietly so Theo couldn't hear.

She seemed to contemplate for a minute then nodded. "All right, T, you win. We're taking Alden's truck."

Chapter Twelve

Dropping Theo off was weird. There were a bunch of parents with screaming five-year-olds. That was to be expected I guess. Most of them knew Wes even though they didn't know me. I should have stayed in the car. One chick was definitely glaring the entire time.

"Does that happen a lot?" I asked once we were back in the car.

"What?" She looked confused.

"That mom who was trying to kill us with her eyes." I'm not sure why it bothered me.

"Oh, that. She probably thought I got knocked up as a teenager." Wes shrugged it off like it was nothing. "And to top it off…we look gay."

"We are gay." Now I was pissed.

"One offense is forgivable here, but two?" She shrugged again. "Let's just say a good portion of SLO County votes Republican."

"That doesn't bother you?"

"It used to. Now I don't bother getting worked up because people are ignorant. Their issue, not mine." She didn't even have to think about it. I wished for a moment that I'd been that together at her age. Hell, for a second I wished I were that together at my age. Then the moment passed.

"That's cool." It made sense. I was still irritated though. "But if you want me to go back and beat her up, I totally will."

Wes started laughing. "Thanks. I think."

We were pretty quiet the rest of the drive except for her giving me directions. We headed south passing all the tourist places like Avila and Pismo. Then she directed me down a small road that led, it seemed, to nowhere. It was cliché, she said, but there was a secret spot, one her dad had shown her. Hard to argue with that. The place was secluded, down a long winding road that smelled like cool, damp wood and sunshine. It smelled like California.

We had to park on the road and walk through the eucalyptus trees that went nearly to the edge of the water. The beach was empty; not even birds interrupted the flash of the sun on the water. Maybe it was just because I was born in California, but there was something about standing on a beach looking west where, with the right imagination, you could see the water start to curve away. It resided in my gut, that knowledge that the world was perfect. I just had to look the right way.

"Sometimes I just want to come and sit here and…" Wes and I had both stopped and stared, the surfboards forgotten in the sand behind us. I took her hand. Five, ten minutes, maybe an hour passed watching the Pacific. "…I don't know…never leave."

All I could do was nod because I felt it too.

We surfed, of course. It felt like we were out there for hours. Just us, the cool, briny water, and the sun. When we would sit on our boards and wait for a wave, the heat would soak into the neoprene on my back, then the cold water would rush back in when I went under. I started to get it. Not just how to surf, although I was able to stand up way more, but why people surfed. That rush that felt like either sex or skateboarding. The waves died down with the sun as it crawled to meet the horizon until it was pointless to keep trying. Somewhat reluctantly, we left.

"Maybe I'll just sell it so I won't have to clean it." The carpet in the truck was barely visible with the amount of sand we had dragged in. I was a little surprised there wasn't any seaweed.

"That's not a bad idea. I told you it would be messy," Wes said halfheartedly. The beach we'd just left didn't have showers so we'd folded our wet suits and thrown towels over the seats. Saltwater clung to Weston's chest and pooled in her bellybutton. A few droplets gathered in the faint blond hairs that trailed down her stomach and disappeared in her wet suit.

Weston watched the horizon and I watched her and the road. The sun was getting even lower. Warm light infused everything so that the only colors were deep, deep blue from the water and orange from the sky and white where the two met.

I parked in front of her house. My duffle bag was in the truck bed with the surfboards. It was cleaner than the cab. I grabbed the bag and followed her around the side of the house. Wes took the bag from me and tossed it into the kitchen before turning back to the outdoor shower.

"If Anne were here she would kill me for doing that." Anne was rather strict as far as the kitchen went. No one was allowed to track sand or anything else into the house, and throwing things on the floor was definitely not allowed. That was cool. I could relate.

"Wow. Living it up while your nanny is gone, huh?"

"Totally."

I was having trouble focusing because her nipples were hard now that we weren't in the warm truck. My hands clenched automatically. I knew what the hard prominence would feel like against my palm. The ache traveled through my wrist, up my arm, until my whole body hurt with wanting. If I couldn't handle seeing Weston half-naked and wet, how could I continue surfing with her?

Who was I kidding? The reason I took up surfing was to see her half naked and wet.

She bent over to peel the wet suit away from her legs. The view made my head light. She rinsed it and draped it over the fence behind us, the one that isolated us from the neighbors. I tried to get my wet suit off and nearly fell over three times before I was free. While Wes waited for me to rinse my suit, she stripped off her board shorts. My poorly rinsed suit joined hers on the fence. She took over the spray again. My gaze followed the water flowing down her body. When I returned to her face, she was staring back with equal intensity.

"Don't look at me like that."

"I can't control it." I was having serious tunnel vision. Everything was light and her.

"You better. I'm done. Finish showering." Wes toweled her hair and looked like she had every intention of watching me with those eyes. She bit her lip.

It was too much for me. I kissed her hard and fast. Just a brief meeting of lips, but when I pulled away she followed like we were magnetized. I waited and looked at her. Her eyes were over bright. It seemed like the sunset had been caught in them except she was staring at me not the sun. She kissed me again. I was going to die if I wasn't touching her. Always. Her hot, wet skin sent shocks through my body that shivered along my spine. Wes's fingers tugged at my tangled hair. I slid my hand high on her back and untied her bikini top letting it fall to the cement.

She pushed me away long enough to whisper, "Inside," and shut off the water. I fumbled a towel off the hook behind her and wrapped it around us. My hands were occupied holding the towel. It was hard enough to concentrate on that because she was kissing me again, so when she dropped my bikini top and squeezed my nipples I almost fell over. We tumbled into the kitchen. My lips were at her throat licking the cooling water from her skin. I worried briefly about the lake we were starting on the floor, but she tugged slightly on my nipple ring making me forget. My board shorts fell then both our bikini bottoms joined the pile. Somehow, we made it upstairs. I didn't remember climbing the stairs or going into her room. All I knew was dropping that towel and seeing her tan, still wet skin. I couldn't touch her enough. Our hands groped and roamed so fast that we could hardly accomplish anything.

She was biting her lip again. I dropped to my knees and kissed her belly, kissed her scar, kissed the curve of her hip. I brushed my fingers around her waist just low enough to spread across her perfect ass. The smell of her sex made my stomach knot and challenged my self-restraint. Her pussy was wet and glistening.

When I bit her inner thigh she jerked forward moistening my cheek with a kiss.

"Fuck, Alden." She threaded her fingers into my still damp hair and pulled so that I was standing. I pushed against her until we were lying on the bed. Slowly, I lowered myself. Our legs intertwined, arms wrapped around each other, and our lips met again. Her hips gyrated insistently into me. I could only return the motion. The wetness made our skin slick so we slid harder into each other. Poised on the edge of nothing and everything, she waited. I allowed myself to delve into her. Her thighs closed on my hand, the hot skin taking me in, swallowing me as she gasped for air against my neck. When she came she bit my shoulder. Hard. All I could do was tumble after her.

❖

I woke to the shower running. My intention was to go join her. But when I got out of bed the water turned off. Damn. I started wandering around the room that I'd spent the night in twice, but hadn't paid any attention to. It was completely normal, excepting the million-dollar beach view out the massive windows facing west. The opposite end was entirely empty, no furniture or anything. On the wall hung three black and white photos, massive ones that looked like they belonged in a gallery. Each was framed simply with a stark white mat.

One had to be a young Theo. He was standing at the low rock wall in the backyard facing the ocean. He was wearing a pair of little boy swim trunks. Small shoulder blades and his spine stood out in sharp relief against his smooth, tan skin. It was odd because most pictures of kids show their faces. This one didn't.

Another picture was taken from the water. It looked grainy and tilted. A surfer was riding a wave with his board pointed directly toward the photographer. I assumed it was Wes and Theo's dad. He was wearing a wet suit and his face was partially shadowed, but he had the same hair, slightly longer than Theo's, and he was smiling that smile they both had.

The final photo was a woman. She was sprawled on the beach with an arm draped over her face. She was awake because she was attempting to hide a grin that pulled at the corners of her mouth. It looked like she was hiding from the photographer. That's why her arm was over her face. It wasn't Wes, although it could have been.

"Is that your mom?" I asked when I heard footsteps behind me.

"Yeah. My dad took the picture." Her voice was really quiet.

"But you took the others didn't you?" There was something about them, a style that screamed Wes. I'd never seen one of her photos before.

"Yep."

"You're good."

"Thanks."

I turned to look at her. Bad idea. She was very naked. "Hi."

"What?"

"You're naked."

"And you're a child."

"That's what they tell me." I leaned close conspiratorially. "But you're still naked." Her neck was inches away and I just had to do it, just had to taste it.

"Alden. I have to go pick up T." It was the weakest protest ever.

"How late can he stay?"

"Noon latest."

"We've got time." And we fell back on the bed.

❖

We were leaving, or trying to. Wes to get her brother and me to go pretend to work.

"So when can I see more of your photography?" I called as I waited for her at the foot of the stairs.

"Are you serious?" She stopped on the top step. "You want to see it?"

From the way she said it I could tell not enough people showed genuine interest, which didn't make any sense. "Of course."

"A friend of mine has a gallery in SLO with some of my stuff."

"Cool. When are you going to show me?" I wasn't letting her get out of it.

"Thursday night?" she answered tentatively.

"Do you want to take Theo? The three of us can do the market then hit up the gallery?" Please say yes, please say yes.

"That sounds good."

My smile must have been huge. "Perfect."

"But, umm, if you want I have some stuff here."

"Do you have time to show me?"

"Maybe one. I think you'll like it." She smiled ambiguously as she descended.

"Lead on." I followed her to a door that I assumed led to the garage except when we walked through that's not what it was. Not really. I'd never seen such a clean garage. The floor was done in black stone and the walls were painted white. A quarter of the garage had a room sectioned off. Some of the corners were taped over with black plastic or just wrapped in black duct tape. Opposite that, long, low tables held an assortment of mat and paper cutters and some sort of heat press. On the wall hung right-angled rulers and similar tools.

"This is my darkroom," she said at my questioning look. "Actually, that is my darkroom." She pointed to the room built in the corner.

"Very cool. Did you build it?"

"Trevor and his mom helped." Built under the long counters were a bunch of wide, flat drawers. Wes opened a couple until she found what she wanted. "Check these out." She pulled a few matted photos out of the drawer and set them on an empty stretch of counter. It was me. Photos from the day she stopped me outside Delma's. I was in various stages of lighting my cigarette or letting it hang from my lips. What struck me was that she captured me. Obviously, it looked like me, but it was more like she caught the essence of who I was on film. I was impressed and a little scared.

"Damn."

"What do you think?" For the first time, she looked nervous.

"I think I look fuckin' cool." She laughed. "How did you know I would like pictures of myself?" More laughing.

"You're vain." It's generally not good when a chick tells you that. "Don't worry. You should be."

"Is that how you see me? Not vain, but that." I pointed at the photos.

"Yes," she responded simply.

"You're very good, you know?"

Surprisingly, she blushed. "So we should probably go."

"Ooh, Weston, do we not take compliments very well?"

"No, not so much." She stacked up the photos and put them away, but she was smiling.

Chapter Thirteen

The first couple blocks held the actual farmer's market with fresh produce and flowers and honey, that sort of shit. The next had food, which mostly consisted of massive open flame grills cooking meat products. College kids manning the grills shouted back and forth in a rehearsed song that only added to the overwhelming noise on the street. Smoke from the grills made Theo's eyes water so we moved past them quickly.

Booths for just about every community organization in SLO followed that, and the far end featured a few more local restaurants. Alleys that branched off were filled with restaurants and coffee shops. Most of the businesses were open for the people crowded shoulder to shoulder on Higuera. Wes pointed out the cool shops to me, the best places for vintage clothes or surf gear or weird T-shirts.

Theo had his own little camera strapped around his neck. One of those primary-colored, kid's digital cameras. He took pictures every few steps and made us look at them on the little viewing screen. Fuckin' cute.

When we got closer to the gallery, Wes called her friend.

"Hey, Trish, we're half a block away." She waited. I was surprised she could even hear. "I don't know. He hasn't eaten dinner yet."

Theo looked up excitedly. "Trish takes me to get ice cream."

"That's pretty cool, T."

"Yeah." He nodded.

Wes shut her phone. "She's gonna meet us downstairs." She started walking up the street with Theo and me falling into single file behind her as she wove through the crowd.

"Where is the gallery?" The majority of the buildings were a couple stories high, but most looked like they had offices upstairs.

"Third floor." Wes turned back to look at me. "It faces down into the alley." She pointed to one of the wide alleys.

We stopped by a nondescript doorway in an alcove off the street. The door opened after a few minutes and a woman stepped out. Her ash blond hair was chopped at various lengths so it hung over her eyes. She was young enough to pull it off.

"Wes," she screamed even though we were standing directly in front of her. "How's it goin,' kid?" She wasn't much older than Wes. Trish threw an arm around her shoulders and squeezed then released her.

"All right," Wes managed to get in before Trish ignored her and scooped Theo up into a hug. Wes introduced us. She gave me the once-over like she was cruising me, but with a more critical eye. I wasn't sure if I passed the inspection.

"Where have you guys been?" Trish asked Wes and Theo.

"Around," Wes responded. They spoke to each other like they had developed a script over years until it was perfect. Not with the subtle sibling-like closeness that Wes and Trevor had, more like they'd dated and found they were better off as friends. Both were oblivious to the frustrated masses that pushed past us on the congested sidewalk.

"Sooo? Can I steal your brother?" Trish waggled her eyebrows.

"Yeah," Theo added.

"I guess," Wes said with exaggerated hesitation.

"Awesome." Trish knelt and Theo climbed onto her back. "Oh, Wes. Keys." With one arm tucked under Theo, she dug in her pocket and tossed Wes a set of keys.

"Bye, guys," Theo called to us as they took off in the direction we came from as he clung to Trish and smiled.

We watched them walk away in silence until Wes held up the keys and asked, "Want to check it out?"

"Lead on." I held the door for her.

The door opened to a narrow stairwell. Wes started up the stairs ahead of me, which meant her fantastic ass taunted me with every step. We turned a corner and continued climbing stairs.

"Hey, Wes." Another corner and my sense of direction was out the window.

"What?" She didn't turn around.

"You look hot."

A slight hesitation in her forward motion. "Thanks." I could hear her smiling.

"No, like really hot." I sounded so smart.

"Like really?" She was teasing me.

"Like seriously." I couldn't help it. I placed my hands on her hips, under her shirt at the top of her pants. My fingers automatically settled into the curve of her hips. Thank you, low-rise jeans and girls who can pull them off. She stopped and leaned against the wall, one foot a step higher than the other. Without taking my hands off her hips, I stepped up and faced her.

"You're okay I guess," she said before twining her hands around my neck and kissing me. Damn, her lips were amazing. When her tongue pushed into my mouth, the sweet softness made my head spin. Those hands played along the back of my neck, making me shiver, lifting me higher. Insistently, I thrust between her legs, our belt buckles scraped together, and the metal pushed back into my sensitive flesh. The pleasure-pain reminded me where we were.

"We gotta stop." She whimpered as I pulled away. Anyone could walk by at anytime, I reminded myself.

"No." Her hands fell to my back, spreading over my shoulder blades. The pressure from her wrists against my biceps kept me from lifting my arms, made it so I couldn't resist when she pulled me closer and took my mouth with such desperation I stopped breathing. Her hips pressed into me, spinning me down a step so my back was to the wall and she so had control. The warm palms left my back and slid down my body. One toyed with my nipple ring through my shirt, sending shocks down my stomach, my legs, up into my throat until it surfaced as a moan. The other hand continued down my belly and I heard the rasp of metal as she opened my belt.

"Wes," I tried to protest before she pushed past the waistband of my boxers and slid her fingers over my waiting clit. Then I just dropped my head back and let her. I couldn't stop her, couldn't stop that demanding touch. She was everywhere. I could feel her radiating out into every cell of my body. I wanted the sensation to last forever. I didn't want to feel her leave. I only wanted her to keep the pressure, that constant perfect circle, but we were not alone, or we wouldn't be for long. Somewhere, a door opened. Wes slowed. It sounded like the front door, the one that led to the street.

Unmercifully, Wes kissed me again and circled her hand faster. There were footsteps. Not good timing because I was gonna come. Wes worked me until my spine started melting, clit twitching, begging for release. I pressed my face against her neck to keep from crying out as the waves rolled through me and I whimpered nonsense and came. The only reason I remained upright was her hand fisted in my shirt pulling me up into her. Her other hand pulled out of my pants and my boxers slapped against my skin. The footsteps were closer. Fuck. She closed my jeans and belt one handed. Impressive. An older woman rounded the corner and we separated looking guilty. The hallway smelled like sex. She smiled and continued past us. We started grinning at each other, and as she rounded the next corner, we burst out laughing.

"Damn." I collapsed against the wall again gasping for air. "What the hell is wrong with you?"

"Me? You started it." She leaned her shoulder into the wall facing me. The dimple in her cheek was showing again.

"Nuh-uh."

"Whatever. Come on." She grabbed my hand. "I'll show you upstairs."

"Sure." As if I could just walk after that. "Like that's what you wanted to show me."

"I did," she said, all affronted and shit.

"I totally believe you," I said like I didn't.

"Jerk."

❖

The gallery was unlike any I'd been in. There were no white walls, no negative spaces, and the lighting was drastic and slightly shocking.

"Trish did the walls." Most of them were painted black or blood red or dark, dark blue. Two of them had massive murals that were very William Blake meets a Led Zepplin album. The ceilings were at least two stories tall, and bizarre, seemingly unsafe walkways were suspended about halfway up.

"This place is insane," I managed to say. Mostly, I just spun in slow circles trying to see the upper levels.

"Come check this out." She dragged me to the wall opposite the door and pointed out the window. It seemed a little weird because normally in a gallery you look at the artwork, not out the windows. Whatever.

Wes started to muscle one of the windows open. It creaked and crackled and resisted, then flew open. Before I could stop her, she threw a leg over the windowsill and sat straddling it. "Sit down," she commanded so I did. It was wide enough for both of us to comfortably lean against opposite windowsills.

"Look." She pointed below us. It was one of the busy, wide alleyways that we'd passed. People below us milled around, shouting at each other. "I like watching people from up here."

The masses below us twitched and flowed with excitement. Dusk was falling, and in the growing darkness parents gathered their children, couples from every age group clung to each other as they jostled through the crowd, and various street musicians attempted to make rent from the corners of coffee shop windows.

"This is awesome."

"I know, right?" Her eyes were still glued to the sidewalk below. "Just wait for it."

I wasn't sure what she meant until I heard a familiar voice. "Hi, Wes. Hi, Alden." Theo called from directly underneath us. He was waving erratically and clinging to a child-size ice cream cone.

"Hey, T," we yelled back.

"What are you doin'?" He struggled to be heard. Trish stood directly behind him as a buffer from the crowds.

"Waiting for you," Wes yelled.

"We're gonna come up," he announced.

"See you in a minute," Wes replied. Theo began pulling Trish through the crowds to the front of the building.

"You guys do this a lot?" I asked even though I could deduce the answer.

"I guess. Trish takes him to get ice cream so I can look around." Wes swung her leg back over the windowsill. "Come on. I'll show you my work." I trailed behind her. "It's up there." She pointed to the very top of the northern wall where huge pieces of burlap and canvas hung. "I've been doing this process where I paint the cloth with a chemical that makes it light sensitive like photo paper. Then I expose the whole piece and develop it."

"That's cool." I followed her to an old iron staircase, the kind that spirals in on itself, that led to some of the scaffolding.

"I'm not sure I like it yet." We stepped onto the walkway. It felt sturdier than it looked. "This is where I display my experiments. Trish is pretty cool about letting me put up whatever I want. You know, see how people like it."

"Do a lot of people come here? It's a little out of the way." If she hadn't shown it to me, I would have never found it, even with directions.

"Not a lot. More than you'd think. It's one of those 'if you're cool you know about it' type things. A lot of Cal Poly students beg Trish to show their work here." We stopped in front of her work. The pieces of cloth were bigger than I'd originally thought. Some were taller than I was.

"These are fuckin' cool."

"Thanks."

"I like that one." I indicated with a nod of my head toward the one she was standing in front of. It was the only horizontal shot of the group. I was pretty sure it was in the skate park in Cayucos. A bunch of teenagers were sitting on the wooden wall that edged the park. None of the boys were looking at the camera.

"Serious? That's my favorite too." She graced me with a smile.

Below us, the door opened and Theo ran into the gallery followed by Trish. "Hey, guys," Theo yelled.

"Did you finish your ice cream, T?" Wes asked before he walked very far into the space.

"Yeah." He was headed for the stairs closest to us.

"Did you wash your hands?"

"Yeah."

"No, you didn't." Wes called him on his fib. "Go wash them."

"Okay." Unfazed, he turned back to Trish who led him to the bathroom. Minutes later, he rushed up the stairs to us. Wes watched him every step of the way. She was gripping the rail in front of us so hard that her knuckles were white.

"Letting him climb stairs alone?"

"I know he can do it." She was still watching him. "It just makes me nervous." She realized I was smiling. "What?"

"Nothing. You're cute."

"Why?" She looked slightly irritated.

"Because you love your brother." I loved that she loved him so much. It was so obvious.

"Of course. He's adorable. Have you seen that kid?" she responded to my half-serious teasing.

"I know, Wes. He looks like you. He's gorgeous."

She scowled at me.

Theo finally reached us. He tugged on the bottom of my shirt and pointed to the images in front of us. "My sister did that."

"I know. She's pretty good, huh?"

"Yeah. I'm gonna be a pho-to-gra-pher," he drew it out real slow to make sure he said it right. "Just like Wes."

"And I'll show the genius of Theo." Trish joined us. "I have exclusive right to show your work, right, T?" He nodded. "Awesome."

"Hey, Wes. I'm hungry." Apparently, his attention span was short.

"All right. You want to get some food?" she asked me.

"Sure."

We said good-bye to Trish and thanked her for letting us look around. Theo led the way back downstairs.

On the street he grabbed Wes's hand and she grabbed mine as he pushed and squeezed his way through the crowd. Wes gave him vague directions until we ended up at a falafel stand. The rest of the night was just like that. Theo would decide where he wanted to go and would lead us there in his lost but hyperactive five-year-old way.

In the car on the way back he crashed out so Wes and I just sat in silence for fear of waking him. Periodically, I would catch her looking at me and she would smile like a guilty kid. When we pulled up to her house, Wes left Theo asleep in the car.

"Do you want to come in?" she asked quietly. I wasn't sure if she was being quiet for her brother's sake or her own misgivings.

I nodded in response. Hell, yeah, I wanted to go inside, and since I wanted to so bad I said, "I'm gonna go home."

"What?"

"Tonight was unbelievable." I meant it too. I wanted to tell her a hell of a lot more. I wanted to do a whole lot more. Instead, I just said, "Thank you."

Her hand cupped my cheek, the tips of her fingers curling into the strands of my hair, thumb tracing below my eye. I tried to interpret the look in her eyes. Nothing. Before she could move or speak, I leaned close and chastely kissed her cheek. Then I strolled to my truck without looking back.

Chapter Fourteen

Thanks for coming with me, Ollie."

"You're weird, dude." She pulled the keys out of the ignition.

"What? You know I hate this stuff." I pulled up the collar on my polo. It was way easier to hide with my collar up and sunglasses on. I was feeling anti-social.

"You hate going to a hot girl's house to hang out with your friends?"

"When you put it that way it sounds different." I hated when she made it sound like I was hella dumb. "Besides, I'm from northern California. I don't even know what the fuck grunion are."

"They're fish. They mate on the beach."

"Why do we have to watch them mate?"

"It's tradition. Stop complaining." Ollie got out of the car. "And get the wine out of the trunk, bitch."

"Whatever," I said as I got out of the car. The window made for a decent reflection so I checked to make sure I looked all right.

"You're so vain." Damn, how did she always know when I was doing that? "I like the new sunglasses, by the way."

"Thanks for noticing." I grinned at her across the roof of the car. The glasses were huge and dark with rhinestones on the side, a little girly and flashy, but in the good way.

"I like the contrast. You know you're all skater punk and the glasses are so not. Awesome. Very you."

"I love that you get me, Ollie." I grabbed the box wrapped in plain brown paper I'd brought for Theo and the wine and barely got out of the way before Ollie slammed the trunk closed. Watch the hands.

"I know, right?" She leaned forward and kissed me on the cheek then followed me up to the front door. Before we could get to the bell, the door opened. Wes leaned against the doorframe. She was wearing plaid shorts with a dark V-neck and she was barefoot. Very Abercrombie. Also very hot.

"You trying to make me jealous?" she asked all quiet and mocking.

"Sorry, I didn't think you got jealous," I tossed back.

"Apparently, I do." We got closer. I kissed Wes on the mouth and kept walking. That was tough, continuing to walk when all I wanted was to press her against that doorframe.

"I guess you misunderstood." She kept talking to my back. "I was talking to Olivia."

"Thank you," Ollie chimed in. "It's about time someone noticed me."

"That's cold," I said as I set the wine on the counter.

Wes walked behind me. Her hand brushed across my lower back and her warm breath skittered across my ear. "Can you forgive me?"

"I might be able to manage it." I turned around to face her. She pressed me back into the counter. Without shoes on, she was a couple inches shorter than me.

"So I'll just head outside." Ollie let herself out.

"I missed you," Wes murmured. It was amazing that when she said such innocuous words they could still hit right to my core. She stepped closer so that our thighs touched. My heart rate jumped and I started breathing hard.

"I missed you too."

Wes slowly pulled off my sunglasses and set them on the counter. "Damn right." She did that leisurely smile of hers, just enough for her dimple to show. Then she kissed me. It was amazing. The way her lips barely parted before they touched mine. How she leaned against me just enough so that I could feel her everywhere.

And the sweet, salty taste that her lips left behind so that when I licked my lips after I could still taste her.

"Wes, can I wake up yet?" a tiny voice called from the top of the stairs.

"Fuck," I whispered.

"What time is it?" Wes braced her arms on either side of me and pushed back. I pushed back my sleeve to check the time, but she got impatient and turned my wrist so she could see my watch. "Damn, I told him if he wanted to stay up late with everyone he had to nap until six." I looked at my watch. It was 5:53.

"It's seven till."

"Yeah, but there's a lot you can do in seven minutes." Her hips bumped against mine.

The sliding door opened. "Grill is ready, Wes." Trevor stuck his head in.

"Of course it is." Wes turned and grabbed a plate stacked with meat. She stomped over to Trevor and shoved the plate in his hands.

"Weesss, can I wake up yet?" It sounded like Theo was about halfway down the stairs by now.

"Boys." Wes started up the stairs.

"Dude, what did I do?" Trevor was standing in the doorway looking stunned. It made me laugh. "What?"

"Nothing. Ignore her."

"Whatever." He shrugged and turned around closing the door behind him. Not much fazed Trevor.

About five minutes later, the commotion on the stairs announced Theo and Wes. Theo ran through the kitchen and out the back door shouting hello to me as an afterthought. Wes and I suddenly found ourselves alone in the house. We had three options: ditch the party and have wild sex, go outside and socialize, or stand in the kitchen awkwardly. Option one seemed the most fun.

"I guess Trevor has the barbeque going."

"Yep." No on option one then.

"We should probably uhh…" She motioned toward the door.

"I guess." The fates hated me. Wes headed for the door and I followed her, probably closer than necessary. She stopped right before she opened the door and turned around. My heart rate climbed to the ceiling.

"Or we could go upstairs and…" That's what I wanted to hear. I opened my mouth to respond when the door opened again.

"Hey, Wes, T says he wants a hot dog and a burger. Is that cool?" Trevor was still holding his tongs for the grill.

"I hate you." Wes pushed past him. I couldn't tell if she was mad or not.

"Dude. I hate you too." Trevor looked disgruntled, but also kind of stoned so it was hard to tell. I followed him outside. It would seem that I wasn't getting laid anytime soon.

❖

Anne and Trevor were standing by the grill arguing over the best way to handle cooking meat. It seemed like she was winning. He finally threw up his hands and gave her the tongs he was holding. Jamie went over and started comforting him, but it looked like she was just teasing him about losing to a girl.

Anne's daughters and Theo were engaging Anne's husband in a reluctant game of football down on the sand. The older of the girls pushed Theo down and took the ball from him. He wasn't very good. Ollie, Wes, and I were sitting on the low rock wall at the end of the yard that looked down on the beach.

"Theo sucks at football, doesn't he?" Wes turned toward us.

"No, he's a genius. See how he let that little girl push him? He's just getting her guard down."

"You're an ass, Alden." Ollie slapped the back of her hand against my stomach. I winced. Wes started laughing.

Trevor and Jamie walked up. Jamie sat next to Wes.

"I'm getting a beer. Anyone want one?" Trevor asked still looking dejected over the barbeque. Wes nodded.

"I'll have one too," I said. Jamie and Ollie shook their heads. He nodded and ambled off.

"So why is Anne running the barbeque?" I asked Jamie and Wes.

"I don't know how to use it." Wes shrugged. "But Trev loves to grill anything that will stand still long enough. Only problem is he sucks at it. Burns everything."

"Anne kicks ass at it," Jamie piped up. "It happens all the time. He wants to barbeque, Wes gives the go-ahead, and Anne takes over ten minutes later."

"She usually lets him do hot dogs and stuff for the kids before she crushes his spirit." Wes smiled and turned toward me. She leaned her back against Jamie and put her feet on the outside of my thigh.

"Crushes whose spirit?" Trevor asked as he strolled back up. He handed Wes and me each an open bottle.

"Yours," Jamie said sweetly.

"Whatever." He stalked away.

"He's just pouting. He'll forget in five minutes," Jamie said. Wes nodded.

We watched the kids play football for a little while before Jamie stood.

"T sucks."

"I know." Wes stretched out so she was lying on the wall.

"I'm going to help him." She started down the stairs that led to the beach. The game stopped as she approached. They talked for a minute before Jamie called back up to us.

"We're not even. Anyone else want to play?"

"I will." Ollie walked down leaving Wes and me alone.

We tried to follow the football game. I was trying to be interested, really. Problem was, football was not entertaining.

"This is very domesticated isn't it?" Wes sat up and straddled the wall.

"Totally."

"Whatever." She lowered the sunglasses she was wearing.

"Is Theo that bad at all sports?" I asked after he dropped the ball for the twentieth time.

"Not usually. He's pretty good with surfing." Wes studied the game on the sand below us. "For a five-year-old, at least. I mean he can pretty much stand up on the board, but that's it."

"That's more than I can do."

"True. You aren't the best," she said. I scowled at her. "Hey, what's with the box you left on the counter?"

"Ohh, sorry. Can't tell you." I shrugged like it was out of my hands.

"We both know you're gonna tell me," she responded casually.

"Pretty confident, aren't you?" She grinned in response. "Here's a hint. It's not for you."

"That's a terrible hint." She reclined back on the wall again. "Doesn't matter, you'll tell me."

"I'll think about it."

❖

Sometime after eating and before dark, I motioned Theo aside.

"Hey, T, I brought something for you. You want to open it?"

"Yeah." There's nothing like telling a kid you brought him a present.

"Come on." I motioned him inside the kitchen.

"What is it?" He asked as he trailed behind me.

"You're gonna have to open it to see." I grabbed the box off the counter and handed it to him.

"Can I open it now?"

"Go for it." Theo was like me. He tore into presents so that the paper fell away in useless scraps on the floor. None of that meticulous shit. When he got to the black and white checkered box underneath, I prompted him. "Go on. Open it."

He fumbled the lid open and extracted one of the high-top shoes inside. "Coooool."

"Velcro so you don't have to tie them."

"And I can skate," he added.

"Without hurting yourself."

"Yeah." He exhaled reverently. "Can I put them on?"

"Do you need help?"

"I got it." He immediately sat on the floor. I helped him pull the tissue paper out of the shoes so he could push his bare feet in. Triumphantly, he closed the three straps on each shoe and stood up.

"Do they fit?" I pressed my thumb against the toe of one shoe. It felt like he had a decent amount of room, but not too much.

"Yeah. Can I show Wes?" He was already bouncing on his toes.

"Sure, go run around. Try them out."

"Thanks, Alden." He threw his little arms around me then sprinted out the door shouting, "Wes. Wes, look what Alden got me."

I trailed behind him and stood at the door. Theo ran straight to Wes and made her check out his shoes. She looked straight up at me. Like the only person she could see or hear or feel was me. I almost died. She motioned me over to them.

"Very cool, Alden."

I shrugged. I don't know how to take compliments. "I didn't want him getting hurt."

"You're sweet." She kissed my cheek very, very lightly. "Theo, did you—"

"He already thanked me," I interrupted her. "He knows what's up." Theo nodded in agreement.

Wes mussed up his hair and let him run off.

"We should probably get him to put on socks with those," I suggested. "He'll get blisters."

"Good idea. I'll go do that."

I watched her collect Theo and herd him into the house.

"The shoes a hit?" Ollie asked from behind me.

"He thought they were totally cool." Wes and Theo had disappeared inside, but I was still watching the house. It was getting dark.

"Wes like them?" she asked.

"Yeah." I glanced over at Ollie then back to the house. "But they weren't for her."

"You like him, don't you?"

"Theo? Yeah, he's a cool kid." I still wasn't paying attention to Ollie.

"That's trouble." At my confused look, she just shrugged and walked away.

"What's that supposed to mean?" I said. She didn't respond. Problem was, I knew what she was saying. I wasn't just in it for fun anymore.

❖

Jamie was sitting in one of those low beach chairs. Theo had totally passed out in her lap, wrapped in a huge blanket with only his curls sticking out. The rest of us were stretched out on blankets around the fire pit. By some luck I didn't understand, Wes had her head on my stomach with her feet practically in the fire. From Ollie's breathing, it sounded like she was nodding off and it looked like Trevor was too. There was no sign of the fabled grunion yet.

Wes lifted her head to look across the fire. "Jamie, I can take him if he's getting heavy."

"Are you sure? He eats his body weight and you have to walk him like three times a day." Jamie indicated Trevor with her chin. They both started laughing.

"Yeah, right. I passed that burden on to you forever ago." She dropped her head back onto my tummy.

"Actually, I think I'm going to take both of them up to the house. You sure it's cool if we crash?"

"Of course. If you're heading up I'll take T and tuck him in."

"All right. We should probably bring some of this stuff up to the house."

"I can take it up later." Wes stood.

"It's cool. Trev and I can carry it."

Trevor woke when he heard his name. "What?" He looked around.

"You're helping me take this stuff up," Jamie explained as if Trevor wasn't the brightest.

"Where?" He was totally asleep.

"To the house." She was still talking to him slowly.

"Right." Trevor stood and stretched. The movement made Theo stir a little then bury his head back into Jamie.

"Oh, look at my boy. He's so cute," Wes whispered to me. I grinned back at her. She jumped up and stepped over Ollie, who promptly woke up.

"Here." Jamie readjusted her arms so that Wes could take the little guy. Theo opened his eyes for a second when Wes lifted him then immediately shut them. Automatically, he tucked his head into the curve of Wes's neck and fell back asleep.

"What's going on?" Ollie asked me.

"Jamie and Trevor are going to bed."

"Good idea." She sat up and rubbed her face with her hands. "I should take off. You coming with?" She bumped me with her shoulder and stood dusting off her jeans.

I shrugged. I was too busy watching Wes with Theo. She pushed his hair back and smelled the top of his head. That probably should have been weird, but it just seemed natural.

"What do you want me to grab, Wes?" I stood and looked around.

Trevor and Jamie started climbing up the stairs lugging some of the gear.

"It doesn't matter. I think they grabbed most of it." Wes nodded at Jamie and Trevor. Ollie grabbed a blanket and followed them. There was only one blanket left. "Are you leaving with Olivia?"

My shoulders shrugged of their own accord it seemed. I didn't want to go, but everyone else was.

"I'm not tired." Theo moved and she readjusted his weight. "I was thinking of just hanging out down here."

"That's cool." She wanted alone time. That was fine.

"So if you want to stay…" her voice trailed off.

"Sure, I'll follow you up and to say good-bye to Ollie." My first instinct was to jump up and down. But that would look pathetic, so I just followed her up the stairs.

Ollie and Jamie were still in the kitchen when we got inside. Trevor was passed out on the couch.

"Why isn't he in the guest room?" Wes asked as I closed the door behind her.

"He tried to take off his shoes and he fell asleep." Jamie laughed.

"Loser." Wes turned to me. "I'll be right back." I nodded.

"You cool, Alden?" Ollie looked at me.

"Yeah, you can take off." I leaned against the counter and watched Jamie try to wake Trevor up.

"All right. I'll see you tomorrow then."

Jamie started climbing the stairs with her arm around Trevor. His head was on her shoulder and he turned to kiss her, but missed because his eyes were closed. She started giggling again. Wes squeezed past them empty-handed now.

"You chillin,' Olivia?" Wes joined me at the counter.

"Nah. I'm hella tired. Thanks for the invite." Ollie pulled on her jacket.

"Hey, if the grunion don't run tonight, you're totally invited back tomorrow." They both started laughing.

"You know I was here every summer and I never saw those damn things."

"Me either. It's tradition though," said Wes.

I didn't get it. Maybe it was a SoCal thing.

CHAPTER FIFTEEN

Let's go." Wes grabbed my hand and dragged me outside. The moon wasn't visible, but the stars were bright enough to navigate the stairs safely. At the bottom I added another piece of wood to the fire before stretching out on the blanket. Wes surprised me by pillowing her head on my stomach again. I started playing with her hair. It was soft. She closed her eyes and let me.

"So this is the running of the grunion?" I asked her. "It's a blast."

She rolled her head toward me. "Shut up. I told you they might not come."

"I know."

"Do you see that streak of stars?" Wes pointed at the sky and traced it with her finger. The cluster ran directly overhead from the dark house above us down to the horizon.

"Uh-huh. What is it?"

"The Milky Way."

"No way." I raised myself up on my elbows and peered into the dark horizon. The stars just barely glinted off the water. "I've never seen it before."

"Never?" She was skeptical.

"Naw. You can't see that stuff in the city."

"Same with L.A."

"It looks hella cool." How had I gotten that far in life and never seen the Milky Way?

"For real." She started laughing. At me.

"What? Why are you laughing?"

"Nothing." Still laughing, she continued, "You and Olivia. You guys say hella."

"What's wrong with hella?"

"It's just so NorCal." Ouch. If you're from anywhere else, California is just California, but if you're from California you know there's a difference between NorCal and SoCal. All right, you had to either skate or surf to care, and you had to be under the age of twenty-five.

"Hella. Represent." I was a twenty-six-year-old skater. Close enough.

"Oh, I don't know if we can hang out anymore, dude. I mean that's serious." I was impressed that she managed to keep a straight face. Well, impressed and just a little worried that she wasn't kidding.

"I guess I'll just have to adapt to SoCal."

"I guess you will."

We stayed like that for hours. Wes kept talking. I'm not sure what about. I was happy just to listen to her. While she talked, she played with me. Either running her fingers over my stomach or tracing my hands. At one point, she stopped.

"Oh my God." She lifted my wrist closer to her face and squinted at my watch. "It's after four."

"Dude."

"Theo is going to wake up in like two hours." She let my hand drop.

"He wakes up at six?" Shit.

"Every day. We better go upstairs."

I agreed and we picked up the blanket. I made sure the fire was out. We hadn't added to it in a while.

"So I assume you're staying," Wes said as we walked up the stairs.

"I figured I'd just head home. You've already got a full house."

She looked at me like I was crazy. "You don't have a car and it's after four."

"It's Cayucos. I think I can walk home without getting mugged."

"No, you're staying." She motioned me inside the house.

I considered resisting. "All right. Thanks," I said. "I just need a blanket." I nodded at the couch.

"A blanket?"

"Theo is here. So are your friends." I shrugged. "Not the best way to announce something."

She just stared at me. Then she kissed me. "Thank you for thinking of that."

I nodded. It was all I could do.

❖

The light coming in the windows woke me up, I think. I turned, burying my face in the pillow. Someone's breath blew across my cheek. That was odd. No one else was sharing my couch. I opened one eye, then the other.

"Jeez, Theo." His face was about six inches from mine. "You scared me."

"Hey, Alden." He climbed onto the couch and sat on my stomach. A bunch of grapes was clutched in his little hand. "You want a grape?"

"No, I'm good. Thanks."

"Okay."

"Whatcha doin,' T?" I had to pee and he was not helping.

"I dunno." He shrugged. "I wake up early."

"I can tell." I reached behind my head and grabbed my cell phone off the table. Almost six thirty. Two hours of sleep. "All right, time to get up." I lightly pushed him away and rolled off the couch.

"Where you goin'?" He followed me.

"Bathroom. Stay here." I held up my hand. He stopped, shrugged, and headed back toward the kitchen. When I came out he was looking on the bottom shelf of the pantry.

"I'm hungry."

"Want me to make you something?" I opened the fridge to scope.

"Okay."

"What do you like?" He shrugged. "What do you normally eat for breakfast?" He shrugged. "What does Wes make you?" He shrugged. This kid would make a great spy. He would never crack under interrogation.

"I like grapes." He thought a while. "And bacon."

"How about waffles?"

He grinned real big. "I like waffles."

"Great." I looked back in the fridge, then the pantry. We had to go to the store. I wanted to let Wes sleep, though. She probably got up at like six every day. How the hell did she do that? "We gotta go to the store."

"Cool. Do we have to get dressed?" We both looked down. He was wearing boxers with little sharks. That was it. I had on boxers with little fish and a T-shirt. Cute, we matched.

"Probably."

"I can do it alone."

"You sure?" He nodded. "Great. I'll meet you in the kitchen in five minutes. Oh, and keep it down. Let everyone sleep."

"Okay." Up the stairs he went. I went back to the living room and found my jeans and shoes. Five minutes later, he came running back down the stairs. The boxers had been topped with a pair of Paul Frank boardshorts. Theo was very fashionable. He was also wearing the Vans I got him. Very cool. But still no shirt.

"How about a shirt?"

Theo looked down. "I don't like shirts."

"It might be cold."

"Okay." He ran back up the stairs and came back down almost immediately wearing a sweatshirt. I was writing Wes a note. *I kidnapped your brother. I'm going to feed him junk food until he is sick. XOXO Alden.*

"Can you write?"

"I can do my name."

"Great." I handed the pen and the note over. "Put it there."

He studied the blank space then slowly drew a big T. "Good?"

"Perfect." The h-e-o was mostly for show anyway. I left our note where it was easily visible and grabbed the car keys by the front door.

"So do you drink coffee?" I asked as we drove into town. The store was the opposite direction, but probably wasn't open yet. I was also going to die if I didn't get some caffeine.

"No." He giggled. "That's for grown-ups." Good answer. "I like hot chocolate."

"Cool." We parked in front of Lucy's. "Come on." I waited outside his door until he unbuckled his booster seat and climbed down from the car.

"Can I get whip cream?"

"Do you normally?" I didn't want to win over the kid with sugar.

"Yeah, but Wes says it's a treat." Close enough.

"Then yes." We got to the counter. It was the first time I'd seen it empty in Lucy's. Ever. The chick behind the counter wasn't someone I recognized. She and Theo knew each other.

"Hey, Theo. Hot chocolate?" She was leaning over the counter to see him.

"Yes, please. Alden said I can have whip cream." He slid his hand into mine and started swinging them back and forth. Kids had no reservations. I wondered why that was.

"I'm guessing you're Alden." This girl looked like she was ready to call the cops. Or Wes.

"Yeah. I'm a friend of Weston's." She was skeptical. "Tell her I didn't kidnap you, T."

"She's my sister's girlfriend." Oh my God. I wasn't sure if I was more surprised or if coffee chick was. Nope, me. "That's what Trevor says," Theo explained in his innocent little voice.

"All right, so I guess a hot chocolate and an iced Americano," I said while trying not to hyperventilate.

"No problem." Apparently, she was taking pity on me, but she hadn't let up on the death stare when we left.

Theo's hot chocolate had more whip cream than milk and the top was covered in chocolate sprinkles. It was a monument to chocolate addicts and small children everywhere. Wes would kill me if he spilled that in the car.

"Do you want to hang here to drink that?" I indicated one of the tables outside. Theo briefly took his eyes off the cup he was carrying with both hands to nod at me. His tongue was poking out of the corner of his mouth again. We sat down and Theo started swinging feet that didn't quite reach the ground.

I had no idea what to talk to him about. What do you say to kids? It turned out I didn't have to worry because Theo was a talker once he got going. I learned about his school and why it's necessary to look both ways when you cross the street and the fundamentals of surfing. He talked so fast I barely could follow. This one-sided dialogue continued through our morning coffee and the drive to the grocery store. He was very informed.

I was kind of in denial about Theo. I liked him, and kids were so not my thing. Even my niece and nephew I had been afraid of for the first couple years, but Theo had managed to charm me. I wanted him to like me. And not just because of his sister. The Duvalls made me want something I'd never considered before. They were making me think I'd found something that was worth the effort. Scary.

"Do you want to help me make breakfast?" I asked Theo once we returned from the store.

"I'm a good helper."

"I figured."

We set a chair in front of the sink and Theo started washing the fruit and placing it in bowls. I watched him as I mixed ingredients together. He was very meticulous. When he finished, I gave him a butter knife so he could cut slices of banana.

"Hey, T." He looked up at me. "When you're done with that you want to help me whip the egg whites?"

"Okay." A look of consternation crossed his face. "What's that?"

"You know how there are two parts in an egg?" He nodded. "The clear part is called the white. If we whip it like whip cream it will get white and fluffy."

"Will it taste good?"

"No. It will taste gross." I struggled not to smile at his look of confusion. "But when we add it to the waffle batter, it will make it all light and fluffy. That way the waffles will taste better."

"Cool. When are we makin' whip cream?"

"After that probably."

"Okay." He turned back to the task in front of him, hurrying to finish.

When he was done we moved the chair again so he was next to me at the counter. I let Theo hold the mixer steady while I held a towel over the top to contain spatters. Whenever the blades hit the sides of the metal bowl he would jump in shocked delight at the noise.

Actually folding the whites into the batter proved to be a challenge. Theo wanted to help, but it made his little arm tired. After trading off stirring, he eventually just placed his hand next to mine on the spatula while I gently folded the batter.

Theo helped me set the table before I started making the waffles. I set up one place setting and he mimicked the remaining four.

"You're pretty good at that."

"Thanks." He finished setting the last place. "Why can't I help make the waffles?"

"Because the waffle iron gets really, really hot, and I don't want you to get burned. Besides, you already helped with all the important stuff." I didn't want him to feel left out, but there was no way he was going anywhere near that waffle iron.

"Really?"

"Totally. You did the fruit and you helped with the whip cream and the batter."

"Can I do anything else?" He was very helpful.

"Why don't you go wake up everyone?"

"Okay." He hesitated at the stairs. "Right now?"

"Yeah. Right now."

"I'll be back." It was good to be informed.

"Hey, Wes, gotta sec?" I nodded toward the back door. The five of us had gone through more food than I thought possible, but hey, we were still growing. The kitchen was a total mess. Trevor and

Jamie had offered to clean up, which was awesome because I hated cleaning up after myself.

"What's up?" she asked as we stepped outside and shut the door behind us.

"Umm, I'm not sure how to say this." I wasn't. Still, I thought I deserved to know if she was telling Trevor that I was her girlfriend, especially if one of them was also telling Theo.

"Say what?" She looked a little worried.

"I'm not sure." May as well just go for it. "See, this morning T and I got coffee. Well, he got hot chocolate, and the barista chick was giving me the death stare." Get to the point, I told myself. I wasn't sure what the point was. "And, umm, Theo told her that I was your girlfriend and that was why me and him were hanging out."

Wes just stared. Her mouth was hanging open. Good, I thought it was slightly unsettling too.

"He, uhh, said that Trevor told him." She'd been quiet for a while so I had to say something.

More silence. Then, "Trevor!" She screamed loud enough that both Theo and Jamie looked up. Trevor looked a little scared. Jamie gave him the what-did-you-do-now look. With a quick shrug, he joined us outside.

"What's up?"

"You told Theo that Alden was my girlfriend?" The volume had been lowered, but not by much.

"No." His eyes got big. "Okay, yes. Sort of."

"Why?" Oh, that tone was scary. It was cold enough to kill. I was so glad it wasn't directed at me.

"He asked me." Trevor shrugged. Part of me wanted to help him; the other part wanted to deck him. Wasn't that something between me and Wes and Theo? "What should I have told him?"

"Nothing. Because it's none of your damn business." Wes looked like she actually might hit him. I didn't want to be around anymore for this conversation.

"Come on, Wes. He isn't stupid. He knew something was going on."

"No shit, Trevor. That's why I already talked to him." Trevor looked as shocked as I was. She talked to Theo about us?

"What did you tell him?" I had to ask.

"That we're special friends," Wes said. Might have been nice of her to let me in on that.

"Maybe that's why he asked me. Special friends is a little vague."

"Tell me exactly what he asked and what you told him." Interrogation. I was at an interrogation.

"All right, fine." Trevor looked pissed now. "He asked if you guys were friends like we're friends." Trevor indicated himself and Wes. "And I said no. So he asked if you were friends like me and Jamie are friends and I said yes. So then he asked if you guys were married." Wes and I both stepped back.

"Married?" I choked out.

"He's a kid," Trevor tossed at me, like that explained it. "So I said no, you weren't married. And then he asked if you were in love and I said yes." The second that final word was uttered Trevor's eyes bugged out and he said, "Oh, shit." Then he spun around and ran. Briefly, he stopped in the kitchen, gave T a high five, waved to Jamie, and was gone. I heard the front door slam.

Wes and I just stood there.

"So I'm gonna go," I finally managed.

"We should talk."

"No, you and Theo need to talk. We don't."

"You're kidding, right?" If I was, then Wes didn't seem to find it funny.

"Nope. I'm out." I turned away.

"Don't leave just because of Trevor." She put a hand on my arm to stall me. "He's an idiot."

"Is he? Or are we?" I didn't know so I figured I'd ask her. The silence indicated that she didn't know either. "Right."

CHAPTER SIXTEEN

There aren't many clubs in San Luis, which was good because I hated clubs and Ollie loved them. Dancing was so not my thing. The pub Ollie took me to was off Higuera nestled between a cigar shop and a punk club. It was a kind of posh hole-in-the-wall. The type where everything is rich brown and burgundy leather that is about worn through and the only thing you feel comfortable drinking is scotch or beer. There wasn't any pansy beer either, just Guinness and some other shit that would grow hair on your chest.

We were there because Ollie insisted we play pool. I was probably the worst pool player in the world. Ever. I only played because I knew she liked it. That and I thought it made me look cool. Ollie found us a table in a back room. Actually, it was more of a wide hallway between the front section of the bar and a room in the back with another bar. People would occasionally walk through from one to the other.

I was leaning over, my pool cue lined up next to me so I could get the right angle, and I felt someone's hand slide onto my lower back with her fingertips just low enough to dip under the edge of my boxers. She leaned close so that half my body was covered with hers.

"Don't mess up," she breathed into my ear. That made me wet, the sound of her voice and the breath in my ear.

"Hey, Wes," I said all nonchalant as if I was so good at the game not even she could throw me off.

"You're losing." The hand was under my shirt now, rubbing back and forth, driving me crazy with those fingertips.

"How do you know I'm not a hustler?"

"You're not." She knew what she was doing to me. My breathing had sped up and my heart rate was through the roof. Finally, I turned to look into her eyes and she started laughing.

"Bitch," I said softly. That made her laugh more. My hands were shaking so bad my cue stick glanced off the ball, sending it in the opposite direction. "Fuck." Wes moved away as I straightened. We both leaned against the wall and waited for Ollie to make her move.

"Dude, I didn't think you could get any worse." Ollie laughed and chugged some beer. Girl could drink. It was one of the reasons I liked her. "Damn, you suck." She moved around the table shaking her head in disgust.

"Whatever." At least it was only pool.

"Stop pouting," Wes said.

"What are you doing here anyway?" I didn't get the impression that this was a cool hang out.

"What the hell do you think? I'm here to kick your ass at pool," she boasted as Jamie walked up and handed her a beer.

"I thought you were here to kick my ass at pool," Jamie said. "Wes has this need to gamble and prove that she's better than me."

"I'm addicted. It's true." They both nodded somberly like Wes had a real problem. "Besides, Trevor and Theo are doing a movie marathon."

"And eating their weight in junk food," Jamie added.

"All right." They hadn't explained much.

"And that's how you play pool," Ollie taunted me from across the table. While we'd been talking, she'd cleared the three remaining striped balls leaving twice that many of mine.

"Dude," Wes was talking to Jamie again, "we have to do it." Jamie nodded at her. They took this shit way too seriously. "We totally challenge you guys to a competition," Wes stated.

"You are so on," Ollie returned. "Losers buy." She saluted the three of us with the remainder of her beer so I lifted my glass toward her then drained my beer too.

"You guys can do the thing where you set up the balls." If I was going to lose, I wanted them to know it was because I was ignorant and lazy, not because I sucked. "I'm getting more beer." They ignored me. Wes and Jamie were comparing cue sticks anyway.

Ollie came up close when I returned with two pints in hand and leaned her head in like we were strategizing.

"Ollie, you know I suck at this." I indulged her by lowering my voice.

"I know. Weston is all cocky, though, so I'm counting on you to distract her." Our competitors were watching us across the pool table.

"Distract her how?" There was no way she meant what I thought.

"I don't know. Be sexy or something. Flip up your collar." I had my favorite jacket on. Faded black, lightweight, workman jacket with just the right amount of stiffness in the collar. "And do that sleeve rolling thing."

"Like this?" I cuffed my sleeves back to mid forearm then popped my collar.

"Yeah. And run your fingers through your hair more." As if any of Ollie's stupid antics might work, I did as I was told. My hair was past needing a haircut so that it hung into my eyes and over my ears. "Damn, dude. You look hot."

"Whatever." Oddly, it seemed to be working. Wes was checking me out. I could tell. They were pretending to size us up. I started doing the same to her. She was wearing tight, straight leg blue jeans with high-tops, off-white Chuck Taylor's. Her T-shirt was the same color as the shoes with a dark red Puma logo across her chest. The shirt was tight everywhere it was supposed to be. She looked good.

"You guys want to break?" Jamie deliberately set the cue ball down.

"Knock yourselves out." I graciously gestured toward the table.

With a nod, Wes bent low over the table and lined up her shot. The edge of her tee came up in the back and I could see a couple inches of the tight boxers she was wearing. I couldn't understand how she looked so damn sexy all the time.

Turned out that Jamie wasn't exactly a slouch at pool either. The first game was pathetic. They totally killed us. Ollie looked ready to smack me, but went to replenish everyone's beers as promised. I practiced shooting. Nope, not any easier without her yelling. All three of them would lean down real low to line up the shot they wanted. I tried that. I was pretty sure I looked more authentic, but I still sucked. I had to step it up.

A couple minutes into the next game, I leaned against the table where I knew Wes was going to shoot.

"You want to move?" She stepped close to me with a mocking challenge in her eyes.

"Naw, I'm good." I pushed my hair back out of my face. Her eyes followed my movements and she started to suck her bottom lip into her mouth. Maybe Ollie was right about the hair thing.

"You're in my way." Her body was close enough now that we were touching. One of her legs went between mine and our faces were inches apart.

"Yeah?" I could smell her hair. The oranges and spice mixed with sea salt that I was now addicted to. I leaned in closer to say, "Good luck getting rid of me." She pressed closer so that her thigh was right where I wanted it.

"You're not as hot as you think." She said it right in my ear then kissed my neck in that soft spot under my jaw with just the right amount of tongue. When I relaxed into the kiss she used her shoulder to shove me out of the way.

"Neither are you." I remained where I was so that she couldn't make her shot without touching me. It worked. The cue ball spiraled off at the wrong angle, completely missing what she was aiming for.

"Damn." She was trying not to smile, but her eyes gave her away. She was turned on and it was throwing off her game. Jamie and Ollie pretended they were really interested in the wall. Music was playing loud enough that I knew they couldn't hear, but they weren't blind. Ollie gave me a discrete high five before sinking her next shot.

I continued to get in front of Wes whenever possible as well as touching things I wasn't supposed to touch while she was shooting, like denim in certain places. It worked. We won. Wes grudgingly ordered a round of drinks for us. She'd caught on to Ollie's brilliant plan though.

I was leaning against the wall watching Jamie shoot. Wes came up and leaned against me like, oh, are you standing here too? She crossed her arms over her chest, pressed her ass into my crotch, and leaned her head against my shoulder. It felt good. I got a little courageous and draped an arm around her. Ollie raised her eyebrows at me blatantly. Jamie started smiling at the stick in her hands. Wes or I would go shoot, but we'd come back and resume some variation of the initial pose. She tucked her hand into the back of my boxers again—I was starting to think that was her thing—and her other arm went around my waist. I wasn't quite to the point where I was going to press her against the wall or anything, but I was close. My boxers were totally soaked. At least it wasn't making me play any worse because that was pretty impossible.

Halfway through the next game there was a scuffle on the other side of the door and a group of guys walked through. Wes dropped her hands and walked away to take a swig of her beer. Weird. She did it again a little while later. My arm was around her shoulders and we heard someone coming again. She removed my hand, walked over, and started talking to Jamie. The third time there wasn't any excuse. A group of women hanging on each other for balance tumbled through. Wes pushed away and put some of that blue chalk shit on her cue stick. She could have come up with a better reason than that.

"I'm going to have a cigarette," I announced. Ollie looked up confused and a little concerned. Wes played it off like it was normal. Fuck that.

All of a sudden, the air in there seemed all warm and suffocating. I couldn't get outside fast enough. On the street, there were tons of people. Some big punk band was playing next door so the line overflowed off the sidewalk into the street. Mostly fifteen-year-olds in Hot Topic punk gear with cheap flasks sticking out of their back pockets. Posers. I walked down toward Marsh Street so I could breathe. I found a decent patch of wall to lean against and smoke my cigarette, but it went too fast so I tossed the used butt and lit another.

I'd found our relationship to be an increasing game of truth or dare. The object was to see who would go the farthest. Who could act the most like we were together without actually crossing the line of being together? It worked I guess, but I was aware of this pain of constant rejection. The problem was that she was with me and at the same time took no steps to acknowledge me. Not that I'd given her any reason to acknowledge me. I didn't know which of us I was more pissed at.

Why did she act like that? Like I was so hideous she couldn't be seen in public with me. I was horny too, and that just fuckin' sucked. Even more pathetically, I knew that no matter how she treated me, no matter how pissed off I was, I knew I loved her. And that was fuckin' scary. Even the anger that haunted me as I walked away was infused with the need for her. It wasn't one of those seeing brilliant flashes of color type of realizations, it was more like I realized, as I stood there angry and sucking on my cigarette, that I wasn't the same because of Wes. I started replaying the last month in my head, trying to see where I went wrong, when it happened. I wanted to find the exact moment I fell for her and couldn't go back. There was no moment.

I so wasn't ready. Or at least I told myself that. Fuck it, maybe Ollie was right.

A group of chicks stumbled down the sidewalk toward me. They'd been drinking. All of them were botoxed to the max and wearing slutty little dresses. Maybe I was being too critical. A few were carrying their heels and walking barefoot. Girls like that always seem to travel in packs. The group stopped and one asked where some wine bar was. I didn't know. She stayed and the rest walked on.

"Do you have another cigarette?" She smiled and pulled her skirt lower. Thank God. I so did not want to see her ass. I held out my open cigarette pack and let her take one. Maybe she would go away. I didn't want to talk.

"Thanks." She giggled like a teenager. Hopefully, it was the alcohol giggling. "You're hot." More giggling. Great. This chick was so straight it hurt, which meant she either thought I was a dude or she thought it would be fun to make out with a girl who looked like a boy. Either way, I so was not sticking around.

"Thanks." I tossed my butt toward the curb and pushed off the wall.

"Where are you going?" If I ignored her maybe she would get the hint. I shrugged in response. "You should stay and talk to me." She giggled again and started walking next to me. Her heels clicked with every step, which annoyed the hell out of me. I just didn't have the energy to tell her to go away so I lit another cigarette and leaned against the wall again. At least it stopped the heels from clicking.

"You're, like, super quiet." She was drunk enough that she didn't realize how close she was standing. I could smell wine on her breath. It made me want to hurl. "I like your jacket." She started playing with my collar. I was so done. Carefully, I removed the hand from my jacket.

"What the hell are you doing?" Wes came around the corner. I wasn't sure if she was talking to my new friend or me, but she looked pissed.

"Uh-oh." The genius next to me dropped back a step. "Who's that?"

"Hey, Wes." I wasn't going to apologize or act sorry. I'd done nothing wrong. The chick backed up another step.

"We should go back in." Wes grabbed my hand possessively and yanked me closer so she could wrap her arm around my waist. I guess it wasn't me she was pissed at. The girl started stumbling in the direction her friends had gone.

"Why?" I stopped walking, stopped allowing her to drag me up the street. "Why should we go back in? To play more fun pool? Or so you can ignore me publicly?" Wes looked at me like I was crazy. "Really, Wes, I'd rather not."

"I thought we were just playing around." She was lying and we both knew it.

"We were until random people started walking by and you couldn't get away fast enough."

"I don't know what you're talking about." I couldn't believe she was going to act like it never happened.

"Sure you do. And just so you know, it hurts, like actual physical pain. If you don't want me then fine. Just put me out of my misery, all right?" Wes stared at me completely silent. The air between us was tangible, punctuated with noise from the street. It stretched and became my world, a world of waiting for her to speak.

"Fine. I'm leaving. Do me a favor. Don't call." And then she started walking away.

She wasn't supposed to call my bluff. "Wait." I went after her. "Where are you going?"

Wes spun back so fast I nearly collided with her. "Don't put this on me. Don't even try. You're the one who keeps running away. And I am so done chasing you."

"What the hell are you talking about?" I asked.

"I'm talking about this running loop of Alden phrases that keeps playing in my head. Kids are great as long as you can give them back to their parents when you're done playing. Isn't that what you said?" Yes, but I wasn't going to admit that. "Oh, and you and I don't need to talk, but Theo and I do. Like you're not the reason we need to talk. Not to mention the thousand fucking times I've asked you something and you just didn't know. Is there anything you do know?"

"I'm sorry." What else could I say?

"That's great. Thank you, Alden." I didn't think she meant that. "Seriously. That just made it all better." Nope, definitely didn't mean it.

"What do you want me to say?"

"That's up to you. You're either in or you're out." She turned to walk up the street again.

"I think we should give it a shot," I called after her. Damn, but it was scary to say that. Maybe there was a chance. I had to try.

Wes glanced over her shoulder. "Try thinking about it for more than five seconds." And then she kept walking.

"Can you just not be mad at me for a minute? It'll be a lot easier to talk."

"Fine." Wes crossed her arms and waited.

"I'm not going anywhere. You want to talk? We can talk." I was actually planning on letting her talk, but she didn't look like she was going to say anything else. Apparently, I had the floor. "I like you. I like Theo. I want to be around you guys. No, I don't know about next month, or next year. But right now, I want to be here. With you."

"Not good enough."

That was it. Now, I was pissed. "What the fuck should I say? You want me to propose or something? Not my style."

"No. I want you to…" Good, she didn't know what she wanted either. "Why do you have to make this so hard?"

"I didn't make it that way." It wasn't my fault. We had to blame that on God or something. "I can't help it."

"You think I can?" Silent little tears overflowed from her eyes and clung to her cheeks. This was all news to me. "I wish I wasn't in love with you, Alden, but I am." She loved me? This was some kind of sick joke. My heart was beating so hard and so fast I was probably gonna die. My hands felt damp and my mouth dry. There was no way she just said that she was in love. With me. No fucking way.

"Did you just say you loved me?" In response, she kissed me long and hard enough that I lost all the blood and oxygen and common sense in my head. There was only Wes in there sucking on my tongue, fingers in my hair, and when she pulled away, I could feel tears on my cheeks. I didn't know whose they were. "Then why won't you be with me?"

"Because you're perfect with Theo and you're an ass to me."

"Huh?" This chick was so damn confusing.

"You have this weird parenting sixth sense with him. You get him to eat vegetables and wear shirts and I know you've never seen him throw a tantrum, but you would probably handle it fucking perfectly." Then why was she so pissed?

"Umm, aren't those all good things?"

"They're great at the moment. And it'll make it that much worse when you take off."

"Who says I'm gonna take off?"

"You do. Every time you wear your immaturity as a badge of honor." Sure, it sounded bad when she said it like that.

"So you love me and I'm good with Theo? Shouldn't this be simple?"

"No." I knew she was going to say that. Knowing it still didn't ease the pain.

"Why?" It came out a harsh rasp.

"I have to think about Theo. I made a decision to take him so now I have to think about what's best for him." I knew how much this was killing me; it had to be doing the same to her. That knowledge, that she would deprive herself too, made me lose it.

"Then maybe you should have thought about that before you took him in." That was so not the right thing to say. I wanted it back even as I said it. I wanted it back as I stood there waiting for a response. Her face fell as it sank in. There was no more room between us for anger anymore. All she had was the pain and confusion that I'd caused her.

It stretched between us, Wes trying to respond, and me trying to figure out how to take it back.

"Fuck you," she said simply. Then she leaned against the wall and stared up at the night sky. "Just leave, Alden." I wanted to say something, anything. There was no way to fix it. So I took off. As I rounded the corner, I looked back. She'd slid to the ground and buried her face in her hands. I hated myself.

Chapter Seventeen

It was loud. The stereo was bumpin' The Faint Remixes, which were pretty damn awesome. A mechanical voice repeating control, control, control over a heavy beat reverberated through the room. I was at some party. I wasn't sure what day it was or what time it was or how long I had been gone. The past couple days were a blur of bars and clubs and parties like this one. It was dark out and the bay leered at me just outside the window. Great, I was still in the city. The only thing I was sure of was that I hadn't been sober from the moment I set foot on the gum-piss-puke-ridden sidewalk.

Lauren was leaning in a corner drinking out of a plastic cup. I wasn't sure what she was doing, but I knew I wasn't going to like it. She was giving me a look that I couldn't figure out, somewhere between I hate you and I love you and you are really, really stupid. Fuck her. I needed another beer. The music was still repeating control, control.

I wandered through the dimly lit house until I found the kitchen. Kegs were set up on the floor and various detritus consumed the counter. Classy. Some dude was pumping a keg in the corner. When I got closer I recognized him.

"Mickey. Bro."

"Alden. Dude, I heard you were back." He held out his closed fist and I bumped my knuckles against his, the type of greeting that says I don't know your last name. "You want?" He pointed at the empty plastic cup in my hand. I handed it over. The music was just as loud in the kitchen.

I straight chugged half the cup of beer. A hand came from nowhere and yanked it from my lips spilling some down my T-shirt.

"You're done." Lauren tossed the cup into the overflowing sink. Beer sloshed onto the counter.

"Fuck you." I stared at the liquid on my shirt. "What's your fuckin' problem?"

"Yeah. What's your problem?" Mickey echoed.

She gave us both disgusted looks. "You"—Lauren pushed a finger into my chest—"are so trashed you can't even talk. You haven't slept in what? Four days? You can barely walk, let alone a straight line." As she talked she backed me into a wall. Her fingers curled into my shirt and she shook me. "You are fucked up." Control, control.

"Dude, Lauren." I was too drunk to push her away. "Headache."

"We're leaving." She let go of me and started to walk away. I tried to follow and stumbled. Her arm circled my waist and she walked me in the direction of the stairs, but ran into Mickey. How did he get there so fast?

"Dude, you can't leave. We're just starting." He joked, but I knew that look. Prick. Checking out Lauren's tits. Control, control, control, control.

"Way out of your league, dude." Then I started laughing. I was fucking hilarious. He was pretty pissed.

"Fuck you, man." He pushed me and I dropped back a few steps. But he was drunk too so I did the logical thing. I tackled him. Maybe Lauren was right, I was a bit fucked up.

He fell back and I landed on top. I got one decent punch in before he rolled me over and we grappled for a minute pathetically. Someone was screaming. I started laughing again. He punched me in the stomach, hard. Asshole. Lauren's red Puma shot out from my right and kicked him off me. He curled up on himself. She hauled me up by my belt and we were in motion down the stairs. The music faded away. Adrenaline kept me from falling down. Once on the street, I stopped to lose a gallon of stomach acid and alcohol in the gutter.

Her cool hand rubbed my back. "Let it out, babe."

"Why are you here?" I choked out from my still doubled-over position.

"Ollie called and told me to find you. Please tell me you didn't drive here."

The taste of alcohol and vomit lingered on my tongue so I spit as I straightened. I glanced up and down the street. My truck wasn't there. "I don't know where I left it."

"Huh?"

"My truck."

"You don't remember at all?" I shook my head and that made her laugh. "You are so screwed. Come on. My car is this way." She put her arm around my waist because I was shaking.

I spit again attempting to rid my mouth of the acidic flavor. My legs were starting to come back along with the cockiness, or rather a sort of drunk desperation. "Hey, Lauren, where are you taking me? You gonna nurse me back to health?"

She released her hold and continued walking in silence.

"Come on, babe." I slung my arm around her shoulders and leaned toward her ear. "You wanna fuck me, Lauren?" My mouth still tasted disgusting so I turned and spit again.

"I'm taking you to your brother's." She pushed me away.

"You're not gonna fuck me? Come on. You know you want me." I held my arms out in an aggressive, come get me stance. I saw moisture fall onto my T-shirt. It must have been raining.

"What is wrong with you?" She looked at me like I had lost it.

"Why doesn't anybody want me?" My face was wet too, and I realized I was crying. I couldn't even breathe. I half-fell, half-crouched and buried my head in my arms. She cupped under my armpits, hauled me up, and folded me into her arms. When I quieted down she let me go and stood on her toes to kiss my forehead. I wasn't going to tell her the story. It was too embarrassing. I was an embarrassment. The story poured out anyway. The whole pathetic thing.

"I love you," Lauren said and then she just watched me in the sick and meager streetlight. "But you need to grow up." When I shrugged in response, she continued her censure. "And you're right, by the way. You are hella dumb."

She wasn't trying to be cruel, just honest. I realized her word choice and started laughing. "Dude, they don't say hella in SoCal," I said. "They think I'm a loser when I say it."

A grin crept onto her face. "Come on. Let's get out of here. You need a shower and some sleep."

"Okay, Mom."

"Don't give me that. You look like shit and you smell."

"I missed you." I meant it too.

❖

Thomas lived about thirty minutes out of the city. We had to cross the Golden Gate, which sucked. We had just merged when Lauren rolled her window down.

"Is it hot in here? I'm burning up." Her cheeks were a bit red. That was odd because it's never hot in SF. Ever.

"I'm fine." We were just starting to cross the water and it was one of those clear nights. I stared back at the city in the rearview mirror. That's the only thing I liked about SF. Watching it at night when I was an outsider. I sank down into my seat and let the cool air and the view wash over me.

"I feel kinda sick."

"Are you all right, dude?" I looked at her again. Her face was definitely red now. Small beads of sweat gathered on her forehead.

"I think I'm going to hurl. I'm pulling over."

That got me to sit up. "Lauren, you can't stop on here." The fine was huge. "We're over halfway. Just wait until we get over the bridge."

She swallowed hard and nodded slightly. "'Kay."

"We're almost to the second tower." I pointed up. "Just a little longer. You can stop at that Vista Point thing and ralph all you want." We barely made it off the bridge when Lauren vaulted out of the car and lost it on the asphalt. I staggered around the car so that I was standing next to her.

"You okay? Where the hell did that come from?"

She sank to the ground with her back against the car. Her skin looked clammy and her eyes were sleepy. "Fuck, I have no idea. I feel a hell of a lot better now." A grin muscled its way onto her face.

"Come on." I held my hands out and she gripped them so I could pull her to her feet. "You should definitely crash at my bro's tonight."

"Maybe. That was weird. I didn't even drink earlier. All I had was water." She took off her glasses and rubbed her eyes.

"Totally weird. You, uh, want me to drive?"

"Yeah, right. You're still drunk." Good point.

We got back on the road and made it as far as Marin before Lauren started looking really sleepy.

"Are you sure you're all right?"

"I'm fine. I just feel sick, you know. But the fresh air feels—" She cut off mid-sentence and her head slumped forward. She looked dead suspended from her seatbelt.

"Lauren!" I screamed and reached to grab the wheel. The car flew off the road slammed into a tree. Everything was slow and fast at once. I kept moving when the car stopped, my body slammed into the dashboard, but I didn't feel it. All I could see was Lauren. Her head bounced off the steering wheel like a sick marionette and her glasses went flying. Everything went still, but I saw it again and again in my head. I tried to reach for her and the pain hit. I looked at my arm, the one I had tried to grab the wheel with, and it was hanging there, bent in a way it shouldn't have been. My stomach rolled looking at it, but I couldn't make sense of why it looked that way.

Everything hurt and I knew Lauren was dead. Everything hurt because Lauren was dead. My head was spinning. It took me a minute to get the courage to touch her. When I tried to reach across the gap with my right hand, my side erupted into hot, blinding pain. I gritted my teeth and tried again. I had to know. I slipped two fingers onto her neck searching for her pulse. I didn't feel anything. I tried again. I couldn't feel the pain anymore because everything was concentrated on the two fingers against Lauren's neck. Nothing. I yanked my hand away, collapsing against the seat. My pants were too tight to get my cell phone out of my pocket so I opened the car door and fell out. The pain erupted on my side again. On my back, I stretched out and was able to get the phone out of my jeans to call 911. Tears dripped down my face and collected in my ears. I killed Lauren. I watched the sky until everything around me went red and washed away the moonlight.

❖

"Here. Let me get that." Thomas opened the car door for me. He looked tempted to help me into the seat. Thankfully, he restrained himself. As I slid into the car, he walked around the driver's side. I was moving slowly because everything still hurt. My ribs were sore and my left arm was heavy so I held both arms close to my chest to compensate. The last time I had broken a bone, I was fifteen and the lime green thing encompassing my arm made me feel like a kid again, but not in a good way.

My brother glanced at me as the engine turned over. "You ready to go?"

I couldn't pull the seatbelt across my chest with my left hand because it was broken, and I couldn't move my right side a lot because of my ribs. I hated this shit.

"I, uh, can't put on my seatbelt. And I should probably start wearing one."

"Don't worry. I got it." He leaned over me and pulled the belt across my chest. "There you go. Let's get out of here, kiddo."

I tried not to smile at the childhood endearment. I fumbled with the little plastic pieces on the side of my seat until it reclined a little and I stretched my legs in front of me.

I closed my eyes and pretended to sleep when we started crossing the Golden Gate and didn't open them again until Thomas announced that we had passed Marin. I guess the feigning sleep didn't fool him.

"Does it hurt bad?"

"Yeah, I had them stop the painkillers once I figured out what was going on."

"What?" He looked at me like I was crazy. I was. "Why?"

"My blood alcohol level was 0.29 when I got to the hospital."

"Damn, Alden," he muttered.

"So I'm laying off the chemicals a bit," I said weakly. "I think I'll try out this whole acting like an adult thing."

"That's good. Good for you. Did the, umm, accident prompt you?"

"I don't know. Mostly. I guess." It was only a partial lie.

He reached across the space between us and patted my knee. He looked identical to my dad when he did it. His movements were the same, even the look on his face.

"What?"

"You looked like Dad when you did that." We had different fathers, but mine raised him. It was odd that he still picked up my dad's mannerisms. We both watched the road in silence for a while, the dark brown and green scenery rushing past the windows.

"So are you going to tell me what happened?" He waited for a response then plowed on when none came. "I mean a couple days ago you showed up at like four in the morning, crashed on the couch, and by the time Lily got home from work. Your truck was still there, but you were gone."

"My truck is at your house?" Awesome. I would have been so fucked.

"Where else would it be?" He gave me that "you're crazy" look.

"I, uh, didn't remember the, um, exact location of it." I paused and decided to fess up. "I didn't even know I went to your house. Damn, I'm a fuck up." I pushed my hair back off my forehead and I could feel it sticking straight up.

"That saves us a conversation. I mean if you know you are being an ass, I don't have to beat you up about it." I caught the smirk at the corner of his mouth.

"So are the kids going to be home?" It was time for a new topic.

"They will be in about an hour. I figured you might want to get cleaned up before they saw you. Lily took them somewhere."

"A shower would definitely be a good idea. You'll have to help me wrap this thing." I raised my cast off my chest a little to demonstrate.

"You still haven't told me why you are here. Last time we talked you were totally in love with the girl of the week and the restaurant was about to open. It sounded like you had your shit together."

The tears rose to my eyes. What the hell was wrong with me? That damn lump was back in my throat and I tried to swallow it. I blinked the tears away, but one fell. I hated when that happened. Thomas looked over to see why I hadn't answered.

"Alden?"

I pulled the sweatshirt collar up and wiped my eyes on it. "I'm fine."

"Liar."

"She's not like that."

"You want to tell me what you are talking about or are we playing twenty questions?"

"She wasn't just like some girl. She…" I trailed off trying to find the words to describe her and failing. "It doesn't matter anyway because I fucked it up."

Thomas turned onto his street and waited for me to start talking. I kept silent until we pulled into the driveway where Thomas shut the car off and folded his arms across his chest. The message was clear: We are not getting out of this car until you tell me.

I gave it a few minutes. My dignity was already out the window, though, so I started talking. I told him about fighting with Wes and the subsequent running away. I didn't tell him I loved her. When I reached the part where Lauren puked, I faltered.

He let me sit quietly for a minute then broke the silence. "Come on. I'll wrap up your arm while we talk."

I nodded and followed him up the walkway to the house.

"Why did you get in the car with Lauren if she was drunk?" he asked as he carefully wrapped a plastic bag around the cast on my arm.

"She wasn't drunk. Someone at the party slipped her GHB. That was why we crashed. Lauren's heart stopped." I made it this far without totally sobbing like a little girl. I wasn't going to start now. I took a deep breath. "She's still in a coma. That's why I took so long to call you." I'd waited until a nurse explained in a painfully nice way that they had no idea when or if she would wake up.

"Damn. I'm sorry." He expelled a big breath of air. "You know we could have stayed, right?"

I nodded but refrained from making eye contact.

"You think it is your fault, don't you?"

Why was I so easy to read?

"I know you are doing your whole self-loathing thing right now, but what happened to Lauren is not your fault. You can't control anything beyond your own actions."

If only I could control those. I was disappointed. And scared. I'd have to face Ollie. Delma too. They didn't scare me. It was Wes. The thought of admitting what a fuck up loser I was to her made me want to drive off Highway One, the idea of her seeing how irresponsible I really was. How irresponsible I chose to be. And for what? So I wouldn't have to grow up? Pathetic.

"Dude, I put her in that situation. Lauren never would have been there if it wasn't for me."

"No, Alden, the only person responsible for drugging your friend is the one who gave her the drugs. It is that simple." I still refused to meet his eyes so he grabbed my chin and forced me to look at him. "It is that simple." He waited until I nodded again then released me. "Go shower. They'll be home soon. I'll find you some more clothes."

"There might be some in my truck."

"Gotcha." He dug around in a kitchen drawer until he found a copy of the truck key. I was halfway up the stairs when I heard his voice again. "You should call Olivia. She's worried about you."

"Okay."

"And Weston..." He paused. "If she means that much to you."

I continued up the stairs into the bathroom and shut the door behind me.

CHAPTER EIGHTEEN

"Y ou got a phone call when you were in the shower." Thomas was waiting for me in the kitchen.

"From who?" I asked skeptically. No one knew I was there.

"Delma."

"Shit." I shouldn't have taken such a long shower. "What did she say? Should I call her back?" Finally, I asked what I wanted to know. "How's Lauren?"

"She's awake. She's fine, Alden." Thomas took a step toward me then stopped himself.

I expected the weight to lift from my chest, but it didn't. I still couldn't breathe. Lauren was safe, but the fear wasn't what was killing me. It was everything I'd done. The things I couldn't change.

"Fuck." It was all I could think to say. "For real? Is she talking? Is she mad? Can I go see her?"

"Yes, yes, no. Wait. What were the questions?"

"Asshole."

"She's fine. You want a root beer?" Only he could go from coma to root beer. He held up a glass bottle in my direction. At my nod, he popped the cap off and slid it across the counter.

"Delma wanted you to call Olivia. They've already spoken, but Olivia wants to talk to you." He sank into a chair at the kitchen table. I followed him.

"Shit. She's mad isn't she?"

"I don't know." He shrugged. "One way to find out."

"How?" I was all ears.

Thomas handed me the phone.

"Right." I took the phone. "I should call her."

His head bobbed up and down in agreement. I stood to go upstairs and make my phone call.

"Not so fast." Lily walked into the kitchen. "Your brother already told me how you got here." She pointed to the chair I'd been sitting in for the last five minutes. "I want to know about the girl."

"Well, fuck." I sank back down. My root beer was still half full. I drank some, studied the bottle, drank some more.

"Alden?" Lily sat across from me, next to Thomas.

"She's beautiful. I mean like gorgeous. And smart, of course. She's a photographer and sometimes she'll just start taking pictures of me when I'm not paying attention." They looked at each other like I was crazy. "It sounds weird, but it's not. It's more like sweet than anything." It was impossible to describe how cool she was. "Her parents died a few years ago so she is totally raising her little brother, and she…I don't know. She's just awesome. I couldn't do that."

"I'm still a little lost. Do what?" Lily was probing. I'd been under Lily's scrutiny before. I knew the drill.

"Raise a kid. I mean they are tiny little people who depend entirely on you. Especially if they were just sprung on you like that." My hand was back in my hair again pulling it out sideways. I was almost used to the pain in my ribs.

"Damn. I guess we need to call our lawyer," Thomas said to Lily. I couldn't help but hear. I was pretty sure he'd said it for my benefit anyway.

"Now you've lost me."

"You're the one who gets the kids if we kick the bucket." He had no tact.

"Shut up, dude." They looked at each other then back at me. They looked pretty serious. "You've got to be kidding."

"I thought you knew. I mean, don't you remember us talking to you about our assets and all that stuff?" Now Thomas was acting like I was the dense one.

"Yeah, but I thought you meant like the house. Why the hell would you give me your children?"

"Because you are great with them and we trust you."

"Have you seen me? I'm an irresponsible loser." That sounded a lot like yelling, but it wasn't; it was hysteria.

Thomas started laughing and Lily was smiling. Not exactly the response I expected. They looked at each other again and Lily spoke. "Nope. We trust you."

"That's it? We trust you. That isn't a response." Why was my voice so damn loud?

He shrugged. "It's not like I'm planning on driving off a cliff tomorrow. But if you feel that way, I'll call our lawyer."

I leaned back in my seat and sulked a little before something occurred to me. "Wait. Who gets them if I don't?"

They looked at each other doing that eye communication thing. "Probably Katie," Thomas said finally.

"Katie? No way. That chick is weird." My sister was fuckin' psycho. "Last time we talked she told me she was going freegan, and I'm not sure if she was kidding. Freegan, guys. That's not healthy for kids. Or anyone." I realized that Lily was trying not to laugh at my tirade. Thomas was struggling not to spit a mouthful of soda all over the table. "Stop laughing. I'm being serious."

"All right, fine, you win." Lily patted my hand reassuringly.

"What just happened?"

"You insisted that you were the best person to take care of my children if my husband and I become unable to do so." She sounded like a damn lawyer.

"Shit. Are you serious? You really would want me?" They nodded simultaneously. I hated how they always agreed. "Thanks. I guess."

"It wasn't a hard decision, sweetie. You love the kids and they love you. That's what's important." Lily came around the table and gave me a careful hug. "You can make your phone call now."

I drained my root beer as Lily left the room. Thomas did the same then rinsed both our bottles in the sink and tossed them in the recycling. He gave me what I think was an encouraging smile and left me alone.

I called Ollie.

"I'm going to kick your ass," was how she answered the phone.

"I'm sorry, Ollie." That was always a good place to start. Per the usual, I was quick to apologize for my indiscretions. I just usually wasn't sorry enough to change.

"I know you are. Have you talked to Delma?"

"No. My brother did."

"Well, Lauren's fine. She's going home later today."

"Good." I let out a sigh of relief. "That's awesome."

"You, however, are in trouble." She used her stern voice. That meant she was only half serious. "I can't believe you left me at that bar alone. And fuck, for what, McKenna? To run off and drink yourself into oblivion? Grow up."

Shit. Hard to argue with that.

"I'm sorry, Ollie. Really."

"Don't apologize to me." Ollie paused for emphasis. "She keeps coming by the restaurant, you know?"

"Huh?"

"Weston, genius."

"Oh." I was too shocked to say more than, "Why?" Maybe Wes did care. Damn, I really fucked up.

"I'm not the only one you ran away from," Ollie said quietly.

I hated hearing the truth. It was so much harder to ignore it that way. I was totally feeling guilty over Lauren. It made for a great mask for my guilt over Wes. Guess that was out the window now.

"I don't know what happened, but it must have been bad. You went on a bender. She's sad. Can't you just fix it for my sake?"

"Why do you assume it was my fault?"

Ollie was silent.

"Fine. You're right. I said some stupid shit. And did some stupid shit. I just wanted…I don't know what I want." I sounded crazy. "I just don't see why chicks always want to talk about everything."

"Maybe because that's what big kids do."

"Talking blows."

She laughed at me, in a nice way. "Have you considered telling her?"

"Telling her what?" I asked like a genius.

"How you feel."

"Oh, that." Yeah, right. "Maybe when I get back." I was already nauseous at the prospect.

"Sure, maybe then." Ollie let it go at that.

❖

I should have been scared because I knew what was about to happen. It probably involved yelling. The worst part was that whatever Wes said, she was right. Actually, the worst part would be when she asked me to leave. Part of me was already relieved because when it was over I could at least go wallow in self-pity instead of having this all-consuming ache. The pain that ate away at me because I knew eventually she would see me for the loser I was. The longer it took her to reach that moment, the harder it would be when I had to say good-bye.

I wouldn't have to wait long. Today was judgment day.

The thought that beat against my skull, the part that made me walk up to that door, was how much I missed her. How much I just wanted to look at her. Be able to hear her voice. It kept me from running the opposite direction. It had been a week since I had last seen her. A week was forever. I had come back to say good-bye, to tell her I was sorry. For what, I wasn't sure. For everything. The doorbell rang and I realized that I'd pushed the button. My heartbeat pounded through me, suffocating me. The door opened.

Damn, she was beautiful.

Wes just stared at me, her stance both defeated and aggressive. My hands were behind my back and I nervously tugged the sleeve of my button-up over my cast. She looked me up and down like she had X-ray vision or something.

"Are you okay?"

The last thing I expected to hear, but I choked out an answer anyway. "A little beat up but—"

"Then I think I might kill you."

"Can we talk?" I held my right hand up so she wouldn't interrupt me. "Just talk I swear. Then I'll go if you want."

Wordlessly, she held the door open and I entered. Wes closed the door behind me and began to walk toward the back of the house. Even when she was angry, maybe because she was angry, she looked so sexy it hurt. I wanted to touch her everywhere and knew I couldn't. My hands started to shake so I clasped them behind my back again.

"I just wanted to tell you that I'm sorry." I launched into my apology. "I was wrong. I didn't mean to say what I said about you taking Theo. I think it's amazing that y—"

She turned on me. Definitely pissed. "Stop. Just stop talking. You drive me fuckin' crazy." This was not going well. "I know you didn't mean that."

"You do?"

"Yes!" She was screaming now. Not good.

"Then, um, why are you mad at me?" I almost shrugged, but realized how much my ribs would hurt so I stopped the motion. It was probably best not bring that up at the moment.

"Because you panicked and ran. And because you…you, oh fuck." She ran her hand through her hair distractedly then looked at the ceiling as if it might decide something for her. The next instant, she was on me. Her lips pressed into mine until it almost hurt. Her hands were in my hair twitching and pulling.

I just let her kiss me. I was too shocked to do anything else. Then I kissed her back the way I had been dreaming about for a week. Her tongue searched my mouth and I responded with equal fervor. I wanted to consume her. My good hand slipped under her T-shirt and trailed along the soft skin of her side before I pulled the garment over her head. She reclaimed my mouth and bit my lip hard, sucking it into her mouth, making me groan.

I pushed her back toward the wall. With each step, I undressed her more, reveling in the opportunity. Her shirt went first, allowing me to suck and bite her nipples while unbuttoning her jeans. The jeans were baggier than the ones she normally wore. Once they were open, they dropped to the floor. I realized that she had opened my shirt at some point because it hung open revealing my bare chest. She paused a split-second to stare at the bruises. I kissed her again and she melted into me. Our chests met in a rush of warm, smooth flesh that made my stomach twist with arousal. The shock wave also reminded me rather painfully that I had two cracked ribs. Wes moaned into my mouth. When my hand slid into her boxers she pushed her hips into me, making her need known. As I cupped the wet flesh, she whimpered.

"Please. Just take it." So I held back. Instead, I lightly circled her clit until she sobbed my name.

"I've got you, Wes. I'm right here." My fingers were poised just inside her cunt.

She threw her head back and whispered, "I missed you."

I filled her, carefully at first, then with everything I had. I went as deep as I could go. Her weight pressed down against my hand making my muscles strain as I fucked her.

"Alden," she cried, "I'm coming." Her body continued to jerk before losing all strength and collapsing forward on me. The steady, fast beat of her heart was all I could feel. Then her skin registered warm and smooth. I took a deep breath like I was trying to suck her inside of me. My side exploded, the pain I'd been ignoring finally making its way to my head.

"Oww. Oh, that hurts." I groaned. I pulled away, careful not to hurt her.

She lowered her arms onto my shoulders. "What? I hurt the broken arm you weren't going to tell me about?"

I shook my head, but that made everything swim so I just stopped moving. I concentrated on breathing because my lungs wouldn't fill up.

"Cracked ribs." I managed to gasp. The pain was making my head spin.

"Fuck. What the hell is wrong with you?" Carefully, she extracted herself from between me and the wall.

"How did you know my arm was broken?" I asked as I leaned into the hard surface in front of me. The room started doing loop-de-loops so I resigned myself to keep still.

"You're not that good at subterfuge. Any other injuries I should know about? " She pulled up her jeans and zipped them. I tried to be serious, but she had the most amazing tits and I couldn't keep from staring. At least I was able to focus on something. When I didn't answer, she demanded, "Alden." It was amazing how much she could do with two syllables.

"Concussion."

"You want to tell me how you managed to break your ribs, arm, and get a concussion?" Her jeans were unbuttoned and her shirt was on the floor. There was still too much of her skin exposed for me to think rationally.

"Not really."

"Are you three? What the hell kind of answer is that? Are you incapable of adult conversation?" Anger banished the concern from her countenance.

I had a cutting sarcastic remark all worked out, but then Ollie's stupid voice echoed through my head along with every circular argument I'd had with myself since leaving SF. "I'm sorry. I got in a car accident. I should have told you before."

"That's what this bruise is from." She traced a slender finger softly down the mark on my ribs. She was barely touching me. I tried to contain a shiver, but she felt it anyway. "Does it hurt?"

"It isn't too bad. I just wanna hurl sometimes."

Her eyes bored into me seeking truth or something else. "Get dressed. I'll make some coffee." She turned and headed for the kitchen leaving me trying to breathe as I sagged against the wall.

Wes set two mugs on the table and sat down.

"Tell me about the accident."

I didn't want to, but I was there and I had nothing left. So why not? Everyone else knew.

"Lauren found me at some shady party a couple days after I left. You know, kegs and plastic cups. So she tells me we're leaving and I was pretty trashed so I followed her. This guy stopped us.

He was acting like he wanted us to stay for the party, but he was checking out Lauren. We got in a fight."

"You and Lauren?"

"No, me and the guy. A fist fight." Wes looked surprised. "Don't look at me like that. So Lauren like kicked him off me and we took off."

"Is it that important for me to know about you getting in a fight over another girl?" She was half serious. I hadn't thought about it like that.

"I wasn't fighting because I was jealous. He was creepy. I was being protective." Wes nodded in acceptance. I launched into the blow-by-blow of the accident, telling her how each bone got broken and how freaked I'd been about Lauren until she woke up. Wes nodded along like she understood. She probably did. And that was it. That was my story. Or at least half of it.

"Can I ask one thing?" Wes cut in. I nodded. "Why did you leave?"

"Because I panicked." I took a deep breath, a really deep breath. "Because I'm in love with you." Wes froze. "But I don't know what you want from me."

"What the fuck does that mean?" She sounded pissed.

"I don't know how to be...whatever it is you want me to be. But you should know I'm stickin' around. I'm not leaving until you tell me to." I definitely wanted to hurl and it had nothing to do with physical pain. She didn't answer. "I don't think I've given you a whole lot of reasons to trust me, and I'm sorry about that." Still nothing. I stood up. At that point, I was sort of hoping for a tearful I love you. No such luck. "Call me." She let me walk out the door.

CHAPTER NINETEEN

How's it going?" Trevor was perched on the wooden wall surrounding the skate park.

"I don't know. The usual I guess." I vaulted up to sit next to him. It wasn't easy to do with a cast on.

"You getting the wrath of Wes?"

"Totally. How'd you know?"

"'Cause for the last week all she's done is surf and hide in her darkroom. And the only person she'll talk to is T."

"So this is normal?"

"I guess." He shrugged. "Last time it lasted this long was when her parents died and she was trying to figure out what to do with Theo."

"Fuck." I was officially an asshole. What was I supposed to do with that?

"Where'd he go?" Trevor asked like I knew what was going on.

"Huh?"

"The little dude." He jumped down into the skate park.

"Theo's here?" Where was Wes? Trevor was about to cross the half-pipe, but he jumped back.

"Duh. You think I just like watching kids skate?" he asked like I was stupid.

"No, I mean, where's Wes?"

"Santa Barbara. Some gallery thing. T's with me today."

"Oh, got it." Trevor raised his eyebrow and sauntered away. When he came back, Theo was dogging his footsteps.

"Hey, Alden." The kid handed me his skateboard and let Trevor give him a boost onto the wall. "Trevor said I gotta hydrate." He settled his skateboard across his gigantic kneepads and unbuckled his helmet. Curls stuck out at odd angles in between the straps.

"That's a good idea." Theo nodded like I was telling him the meaning of life.

"These are itchy." He held up his elbow pad-clad elbows. "Can I take them off?"

"Sure, but if you skate anymore you have to put them back on."

"I know." He was already undoing all the Velcro straps. "Pull this, 'kay?" I pulled at the loosened pads until they came to his wrists. After yanking them off he removed his helmet and stuffed the pads inside.

"You want me to set your board and stuff over here?" I pointed to the empty wall next to me. He nodded and handed his gear over. Without the helmet, his sweaty hair clung to his head in parts and half of it hung in his eyes. "Is your hair driving you crazy?"

"Yeah. It's really long." Thanks for pointing that one out, kiddo.

I shrugged off my backpack and pulled out a bandana. "Here." I offered the folded red square.

"Thanks. I can tie it." He was pumped. "Wes showed me how to do it. See, I got to fold it like this." He folded it into a triangle then back on itself into a strip about two inches wide. Then he pushed back his hair and tied the cloth around his temple. The tip of his tongue stuck out of the corner of his mouth. His eyes were tilted up like he could see through his skull. Finally, he turned the double knot to the side so that it was at the right angle.

"You're pretty good at that." I was damn impressed. Though it did seem weird that he couldn't tie his shoelaces, but he could tie a bandana.

"Thanks." His Vans started bouncing against the wall. I mimicked the motion. Right foot, then left, right, right, and back to left. "Stop that." He giggled. "I can do it 'cuz I'm a kid."

"Whoa. Who says I'm an adult?"

"I don't know." He shrugged his little shoulders. "You just are." That was scary.

"Heads up, dudes," Trevor said from behind us. He handed me a bottle of water then jumped up and sat on the other side of Theo. I gave Theo the sweating bottle after opening it.

"Thanks." He started giggling again when the condensation dripped down his arms. He chugged a quarter of the bottle then slowed. "Trev, I don't want any more."

"That's cool, T." Trevor took the bottle back.

"Can I skate more now?"

"Sure. Helmet and pads first." Trevor knocked on Theo's head.

"Can I still wear the bandana?" He looked at me. I nodded and handed him his helmet. He smiled and carefully put on the helmet over the headband.

"Hey, Trevor," a voice from behind us called out.

Trevor turned around. "What?"

"You gotta help me." It was a kid who worked at Cayucos Surf Co. He got close enough so he wouldn't have to yell. "The bank called. There's some problem with our deposit from earlier."

"What's the problem, Chris?"

"I don't know. They're on the phone. They want a manager and it's just me and Nikki right now." The kid was stressed.

"Go ahead, Trevor. I got this." I nodded at Theo.

"You sure?"

"Totally. I don't have anything else going on."

"All right, thanks. I'll be right back." He jumped down to the street. "If you need me, I'll be inside." Cayucos Surf Co.'s backdoor was literally twenty feet away.

"We'll be fine." He took off. I helped Theo put on his elbow pads and handed him his skateboard.

"Are you gonna watch me?" It didn't take much for Theo to get excited.

"Of course."

"Cool. I'm learning how to grind. Watch, 'kay?" He waited until there was a break in traffic on the half-pipe then skated across. There was a low bar for grinding beyond the pipe. Theo was relentless. He would ollie up and fall back. He was landing like he was supposed to. Both feet planted on the ground. The move ensured that he could have kids if he wanted.

"Hey, Alden." It was Trevor. He leaned against the wall. "I have to go up to the bank to straighten some shit out. Are you guys still cool?"

"We're fine."

"Chill. It's that bank up by the liquor store." He pointed up the street.

"All right. Take your time."

"Thanks, dude."

I looked back at Theo. When he finally managed to grind, he still didn't land it. He glanced back to see if I was watching. I waved and gave him a thumbs-up. Weird. I wasn't a thumbs-up type of person. Satisfied, he returned to skating.

Behind him, a teenager set up his board on the quarter pipe. The kid started down the ramp looking shaky. I got that sick, shitty feeling when he started gaining on the little guy. Just as Theo ollied, the older kid sideswiped him. Theo's hand smacked the ground followed immediately by his body.

I was already through the half-pipe when Theo landed.

Another second and I was kneeling next to him. His eyes were big. He looked stunned, like he didn't know what had happened. The arm he landed on was still under him. He rolled onto his back and looked up at me, his arm stretched out on the ground next to him.

"Theo. Hey, kiddo, look at me." His eyes locked onto mine. They looked clear and his pupils were normal looking. I didn't know what that meant, but that's what people always check for, right?

"I fell." Theo sounded freaked. "My arm hurts." His wrist was already swollen and that was not good.

"Does anything else hurt?" Wes was so going to kill me. I broke her kid.

"Just my arm." He tried to sit up.

"Don't move, okay, kiddo?"

"Okay." Then I realized that there was a small circle of skaters around us. The one who had knocked Theo over was standing there with his mouth open.

"Dude, I'm sorry. Is he cool? Can I help?" he asked, panic-stricken.

"Yeah, run over to Cayucos Surf Co. Tell Chris to get Trevor back here now."

"Right. Got it, dude." The guy took off.

I returned my attention to Theo. "Can you show me where it hurts?"

"Here." He pointed at his wrist.

"Can you move it like this?" I held my arm up where he could see it and moved my hand back and forth.

He tried to do the same thing. "Owww. No, that hurts." The muscles in his little jaw clenched.

"How about your thumb? Like this." I rotated my thumb. When he couldn't do that either, I was pretty sure it was broken. I didn't know if I should just take him to the hospital or call an ambulance. Where the hell was Trevor?

"I want Wes." So far, he hadn't cried. When he asked for Wes, it looked like he was close.

"I know. I'm gonna call an ambulance, all right? Then I'll call Wes and you can talk to her." What the hell? It was better than taking him and finding out later something else was wrong with him. As soon as I gave the dispatch chick our location, I hung up. "Theo, you ever gone in an ambulance?" I tried to make it sound exciting.

"No."

"We're going to. It'll be fun. Maybe they'll put on the lights for you."

"Cool." He tried to smile. "Are you calling Wes?"

"Yep." I hit my speed dial. "I'm dialing right now." I got her voicemail. "Wes, it's Alden. Call me as soon as you get this. It's an emergency." Fuck. Where was she? I snapped the phone shut. "Theo, she didn't answer. I left a message."

"Oh." There were definite tears gathering.

"Hey, don't cry. I'm sure she'll call back soon. You're being really brave." That was what you told kids, right? I was so not prepared for this shit.

"Really?" No tears yet.

"Totally."

"Hey, Alden?"

"Yeah?"

"Will you stay with me?"

"Of course, T."

The guy who hit Theo ran back up. "Dude. They said that Trevor was at the bank or something." Fucking idiots.

"Go tell Chris to come out here right now. Tell him what happened."

"Oh, okay." He was confused. "Got it." He so didn't have it.

I kept up a steady stream of conversation with Theo until the kid came back. That's what my sister always did when I got hurt as a kid.

"What's going on?" It was Chris. "Whoa. Do you need me to call someone?" The ambulance pulled into the parking lot. "I guess not."

"I need you to find Trevor."

"He's at the bank." Not the brightest, this one.

"I know. I need you to go get him."

"I can't keep leaving the shop. My boss will get mad." I was frustrated and this kid was seriously not helping. I took off my backpack and pulled out a notebook and a pen. I scrawled my number down, tore it off, and held it out to him.

"As soon as Trevor gets back have him call me."

Chris looked skeptical. The EMTs were clearing a path through the crowd.

"Just do it, please." Something must have clicked because he took the paper. "Thanks." I returned my attention to Theo.

"What's happening?" Theo was looking panicked again.

"These guys are going to take you to a hospital, T. You fell pretty hard. Remember the ambulance?"

"Uh-huh."

"They're the drivers. They'll take care of you. I'm going to go with you and Wes will meet us."

"Okay."

The EMTs worked fast. It didn't take long to get Theo's arm in an air cast and him on a stretcher. They left his helmet on. It made him look so small.

❖

At the hospital they told me to turn my phone off. I knew it was a dick thing to do, but I left it on anyway. I didn't want to miss a call from Wes. Theo fell asleep so I just sat there and waited for someone with a fucking clue to call me. I sure as hell didn't have one. Wes finally called half an hour later. By the time I got outside she had left me a message. I called her without checking it.

"Hello." It sounded like she was in her car.

"Hey. Thanks for calling me back."

"What's going on, Alden?" Uh-oh, she sounded irritated.

"Well, I saw Trevor and Theo at the skate park and so I started hanging out with them, but there was some problem at Trevor's work so I told him I would watch Theo and while he was gone Theo fell and I think he broke his wrist," I said in a rush.

"Oh my God. Where are you now? Is Theo okay?" Her voice was surprisingly calm.

"I'm at the hospital with Theo. He's totally fine. He was wearing his helmet."

"I'm driving right now. I'll be there in half an hour."

"Cool. He's asleep, but he was asking for you." More like begging.

"Hey, Alden?"

"What?"

"Thank you."

❖

The sound of me pushing the curtain aside woke Theo up.

"How you doing, kiddo?"

"I don't know. My arm still hurts." He looked so tiny in the big hospital bed.

"Hey, the doctor will probably give you a cast like this one."
I held up my left arm. "And they'll let you choose the color and
everything."

"Really?" I didn't think he was too convinced that breaking his
wrist was a good thing. Smart kid.

"Totally. And you can draw on it with markers if you want."

"Why didn't you draw on yours?"

"I don't know. I'm not a great artist." I held up the blank cast
for inspection.

"I am. Wes said I'm a good drawer."

"You are?" He nodded. "Do you want to draw on mine?"
Anything to distract him.

"Yeah." He tried to sit up. "Can I do it now?"

"Sure." Theo was so damn cute it was hard not to smile. "Let
me see what colors I have." After rummaging through my backpack,
I was able to produce three Sharpies. "I got black, red, and blue." I
set the markers on the bed within his grasp.

"Cool." He reached for the blue.

Soon my cast had an ocean motif going on. Red waves with
a blue surfer. There were also some fish and a big surfboard. My
arm hurt like a bitch from holding it up. Between his unsteady hand
and my shaky arm, I had accumulated a decent amount of color
on my skin in addition to the cast. The sheets of his bed were also
decorated a bit. Whatever.

He started getting tired so I packed up the markers and let him
crash. I was beat too so I leaned back in my chair and closed my
eyes. I opened them when I heard the curtain slide open.

"Hey, Wes," I whispered.

"Hey." She wasn't looking at me. "How long has he been
asleep?"

"Not long." I checked the time. "Maybe ten minutes."

She pushed his messy curls off his forehead and kissed him. "I
should let him sleep."

"I guess. He's pretty tired." I joined her next to the bed. "You
know he didn't even cry." She grinned wide enough for her dimple
to show.

"Thanks for staying with him." I realized that this was the part where I went home. "You probably want to go don't you?"

"I don't know." I shrugged. I'd been scrambling all day, but I had no desire to leave. Him or her.

Wes just stood there staring at Theo. For the first time, our silence wasn't comfortable. Like a wall had been erected. I wanted to touch her. I wanted to grab her and shake her until she said she loved me. I just wanted. Instead, I opted for meaningless conversation.

"Did you stop at the front desk on the way in?"

"Yep, I had to show like fifteen forms of I.D. to get in." Wes paused. She still wasn't looking at me. "Wait. How did you get in?"

"Oh, I'm his step-sister." I managed to say with a straight face. "That's why we have different last names, but I'm family so they had to let me in."

"You lied?"

I couldn't tell if she was pissed or impressed.

"I didn't know if they would let me sit with him or not and I didn't want him in here alone."

Wes finally turned away from Theo to stare at me. She brushed her fingertips over the back of my hand.

I didn't know what to say so I continued in my previous vein. "I, uhh, tried to fill out the paperwork or whatever, but I didn't know most of the information. They're waiting for his insurance and all of that."

"I guess I better go do that, huh?" I nodded. "Would you mind, umm, never mind. You can take off if you want."

"I'll stay with T while you're gone," I said. "I mean, if that's all right."

"That would be awesome." Wes brushed her lips across my cheek. I didn't even see it coming. It wasn't anything crazy, friendly at the most. It was the best kiss I'd ever gotten. "I'll be right back."

When Wes returned it woke Theo up.

"Wes," he shouted, "you're here." He tried to sit up again.

"Of course I am, T. How are you feeling?" She kissed his forehead again and gently pushed him back down.

"Not good. I broke my wrist. See." He pointed at the offending arm. "But Alden said I'll get a cast like hers and I can choose the color."

"I guess Alden's pretty smart, huh?" Wes graced me with a smile.

"Yeah, and she said I can draw on it and she let me draw on hers."

"Really?" One of her eyebrows climbed a bit higher.

I held up my cast. "He's a great artist."

I joined her next to the bed and pointed out the highlights of the mural.

"That's awesome." She started laughing when she saw the color on my arm and the sheets.

Wes and I sat next to the bed. Somehow, we ended up holding hands. Theo went on to update Wes on every detail of the day before he fell back asleep. We were as alone as we were going to get.

"Thanks for being here for him," Wes said.

"I was happy to do it." There was nothing else for me to do so I said, "I guess I'll go now."

"Yeah." She wouldn't make eye contact again. "All right. I guess I'll see you later."

I wasn't sure what that meant so I left.

❖

It got cold once the sun went down and it had been down a while. I didn't want to go back inside for a sweatshirt. I had the night sky and the fragmented thoughts wandering through my head, which was everything I needed. One thing was missing, but her absence was becoming familiar, or at least I told myself that. Calling Ollie or Lauren didn't seem like it would comfort me. I didn't want to hear another woman's voice. I leaned back against the slight incline of my roof and stared at the stars. I could barely see them the moon was so bright. The day felt like it had been a tragedy. I knew Theo would be just fine, but all that waiting in a sterile room was killer. Just past midnight, a car drove down the street and stopped in front of my house. It was Wes.

"Hey," she called. Her body was wedged between the car and the open door like she was afraid to get all the way out. "You feel like going for a drive?" It was a peace offering.

"Sure, I'll be down in a sec." I missed her. I couldn't help it. I knew I'd feel better, calmer, if I could just be next to her.

When I closed the front door behind me, Wes already had the engine running. I pulled my sweatshirt over my head then slid into the passenger seat.

We didn't say anything once Wes started driving. It didn't take long for me to figure out where we were going, her secluded little beach. The moon hung low and heavy on the horizon to the east. It was full and white and took up half the sky.

When we parked, Wes grabbed a bottle of wine from behind her seat and led me down the path to the water. It was so damn dark in the trees I don't know how she got us through them. We ended up on the sliver of beach in a wash of silver-blue moonlight. We sat in the sand and opened the bottle of wine with a pocketknife. Wes took a swig then handed me the bottle. It made me feel like a teenager sitting there in the sand passing back and forth a bottle of surprisingly good wine. Her breathing was light and I would have thought she had fallen asleep if not for her periodically taking the wine and drinking.

"I'm in love with you, you know?" Her tone was so flippant that she could have been discussing the weather.

"So you've said, Wes." I tried to match her tone. It didn't work. It just came out sad.

"I've been trying to figure out a way to tell you all week." She looked at me, drank some wine, looked at the sky. "I don't need you to change. And I don't want you to leave. But I couldn't think of a way to make you believe me. I've been kind of a bitch."

I wasn't sure what the deal was with her little monologue. I thought I was the bitch.

"I thought about getting a tattoo," she added conversationally. "But I didn't think you would appreciate that."

We stared at the ocean. Even though the view was amazing, the image fell flat for me. I drank some wine and prayed for warmth.

"So I had this made this morning." Wes pulled a key out of her pocket. "I wasn't sure about it. Would it be fair to T? He's been through a lot." She started flipping the key between her fingers. Was she saying what I thought she was saying? "But when I got him home from the hospital tonight I noticed something." She looked directly at me. "His cast was green. His favorite color is red. But he chose green."

Hey, my cast was green.

Oh. My cast was green. I'm slow. I felt the grin spread across my face and I could hear her smiling too. Yes, I could hear when she smiled.

"Still, I mean, who wants to come home to a kid everyday? I guess that's up to you." She tossed me the key. "I want you here, with me. If you'll stay." That should have been the moment where I ran. Flat out. Instead, I collapsed against the sand behind me. I didn't realize I had been leaning forward, leaning into her words like air.

"Okay," I said without looking at her. I was clenching the key so hard I was sure I'd broken skin.

Wes moved into my sightline. "Does that mean you'll come home with me?" she asked as her face descended to mine.

"How can I say no to such an original offer?" The smile implanted on my face grew. I couldn't stop it.

"You are such an ass," she said, but she was grinning too.

"Whatever. You like it."

"Shut the fuck up," Wes ordered. So I kissed her.

About the Author

Ashley Bartlett was born and raised in California. She is a student from Sacramento and her life consists of reading, writing, and studying. Most of the time, Ashley engages in these pursuits while sitting in front of a coffee shop with her girlfriend and smoking cigarettes. It's a glamorous life. She is an obnoxious, sarcastic, punk-ass, all of which is reflected in her writing. She currently lives in Long Beach. Ashley was first published in *Erotic Interludes 3— Lessons in Love* and is currently working on her next novel *Dirty Sex*. You can find her at ashbartlett.com.

Books Available From Bold Strokes Books

Waiting in the Wings by Melissa Brayden. Jenna has spent her whole life training for the stage, but the one thing she didn't prepare for was Adrienne. Is she ready to sacrifice what she's worked so hard for in exchange for a shot at something much deeper? (978-1-60282-561-1)

Sex and Skateboards by Ashley Bartlett. Sex and skateboards and surfing on the California coast. What more could anyone want? Alden McKenna thinks that's all she needs, until she meets Weston Duvall. (978-1-60282-562-8)

Pirate's Fortune by Gun Brooke. Book Four in the Supreme Constellations series. Set against the backdrop of war, captured mercenary Weiss Kyakh is persuaded to work undercover with bio-android Madisyn Pimm, which foils her plans to escape, but kindles unexpected love. (978-1-60282-563-5)

Suite Nineteen by Mel Bossa. Psychic Ben Lebeau moves into Shilts Manor where he meets seductive Lennox Van Kemp and his clan of Métis—guardians of a spiritual conspiracy dating back to Christ. But are Ben's psychic abilities strong enough to save him? (978-1-60282-564-2)

Wings: Subversive Gay Angel Erotica edited by Todd Gregory. A collection of powerfully written tales of passion and desire centered on the aching beauty of angels. (978-1-60282-565-9)

Speaking Out: LGBTQ Youth Stand Up edited by Steve Berman. Inspiring stories written for and about LGBT and Q teens of overcoming adversity (against intolerance and homophobia) and experiencing life after coming out. (978-1-60282-566-6)

Forbidden Passions by MJ Williamz. Passion burns hotter when it's forbidden and the fire between Katie Prentiss and Corrine Staples in antebellum Louisiana is raging out of control. (978-1-60282-641-0)

Harmony by Karis Walsh. When Brook Stanton meets a beautiful musician who threatens the security of her conventional, predetermined future, will she take a chance on finding the harmony only love creates? (978-1-60282-237-5)

nightrise by Nell Stark and Trinity Tam. In the third book in the everafter series, when Valentine Darrow loses her soul, Alexa must cross continents to find a way to save her. (978-1-60282-238-2)

Men of the Mean Streets: Gay Noir edited by Greg Herren and J.M. Redmann. Dark tales of amorality and criminality by some of the top authors of gay mysteries. (978-1-60282-240-5)

Women of the Mean Streets: Lesbian Noir edited by J.M. Redmann and Greg Herren. Murder, mayhem, sex, and danger—these are the stories of the women who dare to tackle the mean streets. (978-1-60282-241-2)

Cool Side of the Pillow by Gill McKnight. Bebe Franklin falls for funeral director Clara Dearheart, but how can she compete with the ghost of Clara's lover—and a love that transcends death and knows no rest? (978-1-60282-633-5)

Firestorm by Radclyffe. Firefighter paramedic Mallory "Ice" James isn't happy when the undisciplined Jac Russo joins her command, but lust isn't something either can control—and they soon discover ice burns as fiercely as flame. (978-1-60282-232-0)

The Best Defense by Carsen Taite. When socialite Aimee Howard hires former homicide detective Skye Keaton to find her missing niece, she vows not to mix business with pleasure, but she soon finds Skye hard to resist. (978-1-60282-233-7)

After the Fall by Robin Summers. When the plague destroys most of humanity, Taylor Stone thinks there's nothing left to live for, until she meets Kate, a woman who makes her realize love is still alive and makes her dream of a future she thought was no longer possible. (978-1-60282-234-4)

Accidents Never Happen by David-Matthew Barnes. From the moment Albert and Joey meet by chance beneath a train track on a street in Chicago, a domino effect is triggered, setting off a chain reaction of murder and tragedy. (978-1-60282-235-1)

In Plain View by Shane Allison. Best-selling gay erotica authors create the stories of sex and desire modern readers crave. (978-1-60282-236-8)

Wild by Meghan O'Brien. Shapeshifter Selene Rhodes dreads the full moon and the loss of control it brings, but when she rescues forensic pathologist Eve Thomas from a vicious attack by a masked man, she discovers she isn't the scariest monster in San Francisco. (978-1-60282-227-6)

Reluctant Hope by Erin Dutton. Cancer survivor Addison Hunt knows she can't offer any guarantees, in love or in life, and after experiencing a loss of her own, Brooke Donahue isn't willing to risk her heart. (978-1-60282-228-3)

Conquest by Ronica Black. When Mary Brunelle stumbles into the arms of Jude Jaeger, a gorgeous dominatrix at a private nightclub, she is smitten, but she soon finds out Jude is her professor, and Professor Jaeger doesn't date her students…or her conquests. (978-1-60282-229-0)

The Affair of the Porcelain Dog by Jess Faraday. What darkness stalks the London streets at night? Ira Adler, present plaything of crime lord Cain Goddard, will soon find out. (978-1-60282-230-6)

365 Days by K.E. Payne. Life sucks when you're seventeen years old and confused about your sexuality, and the girl of your dreams doesn't even know you exist. Then in walks sexy new emo girl, Hannah Harrison. Clemmie Atkins has exactly 365 days to discover herself, and she's going to have a blast doing it! (978-1-60282-540-6)

Darkness Embraced by Winter Pennington. Surrounded by harsh vampire politics and secret ambitions, Epiphany learns that an old enemy is plotting treason against the woman she once loved, and to save all she holds dear, she must embrace and form an alliance with the dark. (978-1-60282-221-4)

78 Keys by Kristin Marra. When the cosmic powers choose Devorah Rosten to be their next gladiator, she must use her unique skills to try to save her lover, herself, and even humankind. (978-1-60282-222-1)

Playing Passion's Game by Lesley Davis. Trent Williams's only passion in life is gaming—until Juliet Sullivan makes her realize that love can be a whole different game to play. (978-1-60282-223-8)